Shadows of the Mind

A Collection of Short Stories

MANDI JOURDAN

Aphotic Realm

Owners | Editors: Dustin Schyler Yoak & A. A. Medina

Associate Editor: Chris Martin

Art Director: Gunnar Larsen

Shadows of the Mind Collection

Edited by: Dustin Schyler Yoak

Cover Art: "Escape" | Original Artwork by Gunnar Larsen

All stories are owned by the author. No part of this publication may be reproduced, distributed, or transmitted in any form or by any means, including photocopying, recording, or other electronic or mechanical methods, without the prior written permission of the publisher, except in the case of brief quotations embodied in critical reviews and certain other noncommercial uses permitted by copyright law. For permission requests, send an email to the publisher, in the subject, "Attention: Permissions Coordinator," at the following email address: Questions@AphoticRealm.com.

www.AphoticRealm.com

This is a work of fiction. Names, characters, places and incidents are the product of the author's imagination or are used fictitiously. any resemblance to actual persons, living or dead, business establishments, events, or locales is entirely coincidental.

Copyright © Aphotic Realm, 2017

All Rights Reserved.

ISBN: 1981402411
ISBN-13: 9781981402410

For Justin. Thank you for a fantastic year,
and here's to many more.

CONTENTS

Bird of Prey	Pg # 1
Legacy	Pg # 10
Broken	Pg # 18
Lila	Pg # 35
Division	Pg # 52
Fated	Pg # 69
Shattered	Pg # 85
Trauma	Pg # 102
Duality	Pg # 114
Convergence	Pg # 128
Vessel	Pg # 145
Goddess	Pg # 159
Mother	Pg # 171
About the Author	Pg # 178

BIRD OF PREY

Marks like this one were the reason Ravenna sometimes regretted the path her life had taken. Maybe she could have been a writer, like her mother. A police officer, like her father. She could have been like Aunt Clarisse, who had worked for President Hartley and been forced to drop off the radar after false accusations and scandals. At least with any of these, Ravenna could have said she had made a decision to be proud of. Her mother told stories she loved and shared them with the world; her father strived to protect people; her aunt had done the noble thing, taking the fall for a government fiasco, preserving the reputation of her employer and close friend.

Instead, Ravenna thought as she drifted through the sidewalks of Chicago, her black jacket pulled tight around her in the cold drizzle, *I ran. I was selfish.* She liked to believe selfishness wasn't what had driven her to leave, but that was wishful thinking. Had she not been selfish, she would have gone home by now.

Ravenna glanced over the street as a passing pair of hovercar headlights cut through the darkness. In the instant of illumination, she caught sight of her quarry. The woman was several yards ahead– far enough for Ravenna to remain concealed.

The mark's name was irrelevant. In fact, Ravenna was making a concentrated effort not to remember it. If she saw them all as humans, it would be a lot more difficult to convince herself to kill them.

Even when she had left home, she hadn't imagined herself becoming a killer. After all, death was what she had fled to escape.

***

Her head snapped upward at the sound of the cracking ice, her focus torn from the skates on which she waddled unsteadily toward the lake. Her hazel eyes fell on her brother. He looked to her in panic. A moment later, he slipped through the ice and into the dark water beneath.

***

The image was as clear to her now as it had been on the day it had happened. She used to pray that it would fade from her memory, at least a little, but the scene had returned to her in her dreams or in a crowded classroom or out with her friends, without fail. Eventually, she had stopped praying altogether. She could survive on her own.

I needed to get away, she told herself now as she turned a corner, losing sight of her mark for only an instant. *I would have gone insane.*

Just last week, she had taken down three marks in the course of two days. The first had been a drug dealer, and judging by the sum of money she'd received for putting a bullet through his skull, her employer had been one as well. Not that she'd asked. A certain level of anonymity was required in the business of murder, and the less everyone involved knew about one another, the better. It was harder to be double-crossed if personal information was kept to a minimum.

The corner of Ravenna's mouth twitched up into a cold, bitter smile. Of course she knew this now, but it would have been much more helpful ten years ago.

***

Chicago should have been more like New York, Ravenna decided as she wandered the city for the third night since her arrival, alone on Navy Pier. The buildings were tall and the city was crowded, with its chrome towers and layers of hovercars claiming the streets, but it wasn't home. Lake Michigan was beautiful; she watched the dark water ripple just off the pier, and glint in the moonlight that fell from overhead, but it wasn't the Hudson River, where she had often gone boating with her family as a child.

You chose this, she told herself, shaking her head and zipping up her pale green jacket to shield herself from the wind. *You aren't allowed to complain.*

Ravenna yawned, turning away from the dark water and starting toward her temporary home a few blocks from the pier. Living in a hotel hadn't been the plan, but for now, it was good enough. She watched the hovercars pass and wondered how many people lived here and how many had done so all their lives. She wondered if she would ever stop feeling out of place.

"Presenting the future of robotics technology," a smooth female voice announced from a screen in a store window to Ravenna's left, "the seventh generation Adam and Eve from Genesis Tech."

Ravenna paused to glance at the screen, where a blond man and a red-haired woman smiled at the audience. As they approached the camera, their movements were fluid and realistic. They were dressed in a closely-tailored grey suit and dress, respectively, and while Ravenna remembered the last generation of Genesis androids being rather stiff and inhuman, she thought these two could pass well for a living man and woman.

"Arriving Fall 2218," said the announcer's voice. "Each model can be purchased for the unbelievably low price of—"

"Hey, sweetheart."

Ravenna's mouth went dry, her muscles tensing from a sickening pang of fear. The voice was at her ear. She hadn't been paying enough attention to notice anyone approaching. She said nothing. Strong arms enclosed her and pulled her backward. A hand slipped over her mouth and she felt the cold barrel of a plasma gun pressing into her side. Her first instinct had been to scream for help, but if she made noise, she would certainly be shot. She thought she knew enough about self-defense to attempt to fight, but she couldn't think clearly enough in her panic to form a plan.

Her captor hauled her into a nearby alley and shoved her hard against the wall of an apartment building. He eyed her up and down, and a wicked grin curled his lips. He pressed his forearm across her throat to pin her to the wall, and as a choked breath left her lungs, she glanced down to see the gun only inches from her face. Her heart pounded loudly in her ears, and she couldn't think. His free hand ripped the zipper of her jacket downward, and her stomach twisted.

"Please," she gasped, reaching up to attempt to pry his arm from her throat.

"Shut up."

He wrestled her jacket from her shoulders as she struggled against him, and in a moment of pure panic, she kicked him hard in the shin. He hissed in pain and pressed the gun to her temple, his dark eyes filled with malice.

"Shouldn't have done that."

A gunshot echoed through the alley, and Ravenna realized only several seconds after the sound had faded that she had closed her eyes tightly. She forced herself to open them, and she registered slowly that there was no longer the suffocating pressure on her throat, and the pounding in her ears was the only remaining sign of her terrifying predicament. Except, that was, for the man lying at her feet. He was facing the ground, and a plasma bolt had landed perfectly in the center of the back of his head.

Ravenna dropped to the ground, her head in her hands as she struggled to get her breathing back under her control. Her hyperventilating nearly drowned out the sound of feet clamoring down the ladder across the alley and rushing across the pavement toward her.

A hand rested gently on her elbow. "Are you hurt?"

Ravenna lifted her face to see another man crouching beside her. Unlike the first, his eyes were not malicious. They were green, and while there was a sense of severity about his face, his expression made him seem like someone who had witnessed a lot of suffering, not one who enjoyed inflicting it. Regardless, his shot suggested a practiced marksman.

"I'm fine. Um… thank you." Ravenna inhaled deeply and let out her breath in a sigh, trying to rid herself of her shock and nerves. She was safe. Probably.

The man nodded. "You're lucky he was such an ass. If he hadn't done this and worse a million times, I wouldn't have been hired."

"Hired?" she repeated blankly, not understanding.

"Come on. We'll talk when we're farther away, if you want." He offered her a hand, and after a moment's hesitation, she took it.

It might be insane, she thought as he helped her to her feet. *He just killed a man. But he also just saved my life. And I don't want to be here when someone finds the body.* She followed the man out of the alley, pulling on her jacket once more to shut out the cold night air and keep herself from shivering more than she already was.

"I'm Roman, by the way."

She looked up at him. Roman had dark brown hair that was still several shades lighter than hers, and he was dressed in black. He appeared to be a few years older than her; he might have been in his early twenties. His clothing and the deftness of his movements suggested that he was accustomed to blending into the darkness around him.

"Ravenna," she said simply in introduction. "Why were you hired?"

Roman smiled. "You sure you want to know?"

"You saved me. You got my attention. I want to know."

"I get paid to kill people who deserve it."

Ravenna frowned, folding her arms over her chest as she considered his words and worked to keep pace with his longer strides. She had always viewed murder as undeniably wrong and those who committed it as irredeemably guilty. But Roman had saved her.

"Why?"

Roman said nothing immediately, and when Ravenna looked up at him again, his brows were pulled together thoughtfully. "I've seen a lot of people get away with things they shouldn't have."

***

Perhaps, Ravenna thought now as she walked more quickly to close the distance somewhat between herself and the woman she had been hired to kill, she had decided to follow Roman's path in order to punish herself. She felt responsible for the death of someone she cared for, and there weren't many people to care for, in the life of an assassin. Roman was the only one she had ever been close to, since she had left New York. He had taught her everything he knew– how to aim and fire a plasma gun, how to remain hidden, how to judge whether she had been tricked into pursuing a target she did not feel justified in attacking.

Just as Roman had, Ravenna had elected only to pursue marks who had committed crimes. She had turned down countless potential employers over the last decade who had tried to hire her to kill for personal reasons. Estranged spouses who wanted insurance money or revenge, politicians who wanted more power... Ravenna wanted no part in petty hits. She saw herself as an agent of justice, or at least of karma, and once in a while, this allowed her to sleep at night.

This mark, though, wasn't exactly one of her normal targets. The woman had been accused of embezzling a large sum of money from a banking firm to an illegal organization Ravenna hadn't been able to gather much information about, but in her tailing of the woman for the last several days, she had not seen any evidence of her guilt. The woman didn't appear to be involved with the organization at all, and though she kept expecting evidence to turn up to the contrary, nothing happened.

Her employer must have been talented at forgery. The ledgers and transfer documents, Ravenna concluded, had been falsified. She turned a corner and abandoned her pursuit.

***

"Are you sure about this?" Ravenna glanced nervously over her shoulder, certain that she and Roman were being watched.

"Yes. I'm not going to take out a mark who isn't guilty, Rae. Wait here for me, and I'll be back in a minute. And remember: if I'm not—"

"I get the hell out of here and I never met you."

"Right." Roman grinned, reaching out to squeeze Ravenna's shoulder before turning away and making for the corner of Elston and Chestnut, several buildings away.

Sighing heavily, Ravenna reclined against the wall she stood beside and surveyed the area through her dark sunglasses. The man he had been hired to kill had, Roman determined, not been guilty of the crime of which he was accused. The employer had insisted Roman meet him in person, and Ravenna had anticipated something going wrong instantly.

She glanced to her left to see that a black-coated woman had arrived and was speaking with Roman. The woman's face was calm, and neither moved much as they spoke. Roman was accustomed to avoiding attention, and Ravenna suspected the woman was, as well. Ravenna looked away at the sound of a barking dog from her right, and she allowed herself to smile for a moment as she watched a small boy lead a very large yellow lab while his parents followed.

A gunshot pierced the moment of calm observation, and Ravenna whipped around to face the street corner where she had last seen Roman.

Clutching his chest, he fell to the ground as the woman disappeared around the corner. Ravenna whipped out her gun as she hurtled toward her friend. She crouched beside him. The plasma bolt had hit him in the chest, and he was struggling to breathe. Pushing herself to her feet, she ran at full speed after the retreating, black-coated woman, gun drawn. She stopped in her tracks as the wail of police sirens reached her ears. Two Chicago P.D. hovercars approached, and as her heart plummeted sickeningly, she realized how bad this would look. She was running from the scene with a gun. Sighing in frustration and helplessness, she returned to Roman, who was coughing blood onto the sidewalk. Ravenna crouched beside him.

"Roman. Come on, I'm going to lift you and we're going to get out of here." He opened his eyes and frowned at her.

"Run."

"I'm not leaving–"

"Go!"

***

She had barely managed to escape before the police had

converged on the corner. Every day since, she had wondered what had become of him and had been unable to find out.

Now, as she ascended the steps to the apartment her current employer had told her to visit if there was a problem, Ravenna wondered if Roman would be proud of what she had done since she had last seen him. She had continued punishing the guilty, and today, she had spared one who was potentially innocent, just as he would have done.

Maybe I'm not completely selfish, she thought as she knocked on the door. *I could have just done it and taken the money.*

The door opened, and Ravenna trained her eyes on the welcome mat. "I couldn't complete the hit."

"Why not?" Her employer's voice was cold and female, just as it had been on the phone.

"She was innocent." Sighing, Ravenna looked up to meet the woman's eyes at last, and she froze, unable to speak.

It was the woman who had shot Roman.

"I pay you people to kill, not to make judgments." The woman glared, and she reached into her coat. Ravenna saw a glint of silver within.

Ravenna pulled her own gun from its holster and fired, hitting the woman squarely in the forehead.

She turned away without pause and started down the stairs. No amount of money could have compared to her satisfaction.

LEGACY

Clarisse glared at the list of names projected above the holofile on her desk. She'd been studying the list for the better part of an hour, and no matter how she tried to shake the beginnings of a bad idea from her mind, she couldn't entirely rid herself of it.

The words *"Known Assassins' Guilds"* glared ominously up at her from the top of the readout hovering several inches above the smooth, flat silver screen. Clarisse flicked the right edge of the projection, and its title disappeared to give way to more items on the list as the cursor scrolled downward.

I don't want the help of any of these. Caedis, Laurea, Viperae… Clarisse shook her head. *They can't be trusted. How did we get to the point that we can't stop the guilds, anyway? How did we lose that much power?*

As she surveyed the names, she fiddled absently with the small chain links of the gold bracelet on her left wrist. She remembered the day she'd given one just like it to her niece, who had, as a child, wanted to follow in her footsteps and work for the government. Clarisse had brought Ravenna along on several visits to the White House when she'd been Senior Advisor to President

Hartley, and now that she had been reassigned to head an organization that was far more trouble than it was worth, Clarisse found her thoughts returning to her niece again.

Would she want to be part of this? Could I even tell her I was the one hiring her? I would have to arrange something. I'd be drawing attention to her; I have to make sure she's protected.

Clarisse skimmed the list for a few seconds longer without seeing a word projected, and then she pulled in a quick breath and pushed herself backward from her desk. She slid to her feet, and her chair bobbed slightly where it hovered just above the floor at the loss of her weight. She rolled her shoulders backward, smoothed out her skirt, and kept her hold on the holofile as she strode out of her office and down the corridor.

The walls on either side of her path were lined with paintings that had been considered antique for hundreds of years; former leaders stared somberly out at the hallway. Clarisse refused to allow her eyes to linger on any of them for too long. She doubted most of them would have allowed their nation to be put into this position in the first place.

When she reached the door she sought, Clarisse pulled in a long breath and knocked.

"Yes?" called the voice of President Isabella Hartley from the other side.

"It's Clarisse, ma'am."

"Come in."

Clarisse pushed open the door and entered the Oval Office. Isabella sat at her desk, her hands folded, and her long red hair pulled back into a tight bun.

"Have you had any luck solving our problem?" Isabella asked.

"Somewhat, Madam President," said Clarisse. "As you know, my niece is... ah..."

"She's run into trouble with the law?" Isabella supplied.

Clarisse's cheeks burned. "Yes, ma'am."

"Where is she, now? Still in Chicago? Did she align

with one of the guilds?"

"No. She works alone." Clarisse pulled in a long breath and let it out again. "Madam President," she continued, "I've thought about this for weeks, since your proposal that we enlist a guild to take the Seven down. I think we would stand a better chance of remaining off the radar if we hire lone assassins. People who won't draw attention because they choose not to be found even by others like them. If they succeed, word won't spread, and if they fail—" The words died in Clarisse's throat. She refused to allow herself to picture Ravenna failing at such a dangerous game.

When Clarisse said nothing for a few moments, Isabella spoke again.

"You want her to be one of them?" she asked, raising a red brow.

Clarisse swallowed, her fingers moving to her bracelet on reflex. "I know Ravenna's capable," she said. "I only waited this long because I worry about her. I decided I trust her to do it and keep herself safe."

Isabella glanced to the photoscroll on her desk. Though it was facing away from Clarisse, she knew it contained a series of images of Isabella's family programmed to play on a loop.

Isabella, no doubt, was thinking about her daughter, who was Ravenna's age.

"In exchange, I'd want her pardoned," said Clarisse. "For everything. Off the record."

Isabella's eyes flicked back to meet Clarisse's, her mouth pressed into a tight line.

"I knew it would be something like that," Isabella muttered.

"She's made mistakes. I just… I think she can change—can stop going down this path. And when she does, I want her to be able to put it all behind her. Please, Madam President. I've done everything you've asked of me."

I gave up my real job as your advisor to head the Division. And now the blood of everyone those androids have killed is on my hands, Clarisse wanted to say.

Isabella watched her, and Clarisse kept all her focus on remaining still and slowing the thrum of her pulse. At last, Isabella sighed.

"Fine," she said. "An unofficial pardon in exchange for one of them being silenced." She held out her hand. "You have my word."

Relief crashed over Clarisse, and she grabbed Isabella's hand a bit more firmly than she'd intended.

"Thank you, ma'am. Thank you."

***

Everything about this hit felt wrong.

Ravenna had been hired to take out a target in Washington, D.C. Her rational side had screamed at her not to agree, as the odds of being caught were considerably higher here than most any other place she could have gone. But her heart had become hollow, and she had nothing to lose. The only thing of any value to her was on her wrist, tucked beneath the arm of the black sweater she'd chosen to block out the biting wind. She'd received the bracelet from her aunt Clarisse before leaving home as soon as she'd graduated high school. It was the twin to Clarisse's own, and the reminder of the relative Ravenna had always admired most was welcome, when she hadn't seen anyone in her family for years.

As though the overwhelming presence of the law in the city had not been difficult enough to navigate to get to the spot her mark was supposed to be, the lack of information provided by her employer complicated matters. Ravenna knew nothing about the man she was to kill apart from his name. No history, no justification for what she planned to do.

When choosing her clients over the years, she had elected to gravitate toward the targets that were guilty of one thing or another. It helped her sleep at night to know that some good might come of her actions, if only in the form of the prevention of future wrongs. She viewed herself as an agent of karma.

Now, however, things were different. She had no idea who the man known only as "Ra" really was, only that she was tasked with killing him.

Ravenna leaned against a wall in an alleyway, awaiting her moment of opportunity as she blended into the darkness. Her target was expected to pass this way within the hour, if her information was correct. The shops nearby had all closed for the night, and so far, Ravenna had only seen a few sets of headlights pass.

A group of tourists drifted down the sidewalk in front of the alley, chatting loudly. They looked around the right age to be high school students, and Ravenna's chest clenched at the sight of them.

"Let's hope someone doesn't get herself separated from the group again tomorrow," said one of the passersby, poking her companion in the shoulder.

"It wasn't my fault! I left my phone at the hotel! I wanted to call you, but I couldn't. Besides, the one time I was actually lost, none of you realized it until I showed up again and scared the hell out of you."

"The flight simulator was incredible," said a boy walking behind the first pair.

"It was," said the girl beside him with a nod. "I still can't believe you let me work the guns."

Their voices gradually faded, their words mingled with laughter.

They're happy.

Ravenna wished more than anything to return to that age. In just a few short years, she'd lost everything she'd loved about her life, and there were days she couldn't recognize herself in the mirror. She couldn't recall the last time she had been genuinely happy.

After the group's voices had deserted the area, a lone

figure passed, his hands in his pockets and his vision directed toward the sidewalk.

Several seconds after he was clear of the alley, Ravenna slipped silently into the street after him. Her feet fell on the pavement in precise time with his, and she had almost convinced herself that things would go according to plan.

"You're not bad at this," said the man.

Ravenna's heart leapt into her throat.

"Not fantastic, but not bad."

The man turned to face her, and his features were caught in the glow of a streetlamp. His skin was olive, and his dark hair was pulled back behind his head. His eyes were a startlingly bright shade of green, and they held a kind of dark fire she had never seen.

She reached for the plasma gun at her side and drew it in a flash. Returning her attention to where her target should have been, she found that he had disappeared. She scowled and opened her mouth, but before she could make a sound, she heard his voice at her ear.

"Right here."

Ravenna jumped, whipping around to face him. She pointed the gun at his heart, and he slid to the side and into the next alley more quickly than she had ever seen anyone move.

"Not fantastic," he said.

The taunts and the fear surging through Ravenna set her on edge. She fought to remain focused. To anticipate.

I can't fire until I get a shot. The second I do, cops will be on their way, and I can't leave until I take him down.

She trained the gun on him for a second time, and again he evaded her, moving in a blur farther down the alley.

What the hell? He can't be human. Why would someone hire me to take down an android?

"Do you have any idea who I am?" Ra demanded. "You're out of your depth."

Ravenna charged toward him, her weapon raised. As

Ra surged forward in an attempt to slip past her, Ravenna swung out her leg, focusing all her energy on tripping him.

Ra stumbled but did not fall. He caught Ravenna by the wrist, and her muscles screamed and strained as he used his grip on her to toss her toward the street. She threw out her free hand to catch herself. Her palm seared as it snagged on the sidewalk.

Ravenna forced herself to her feet and started into the alley after her target.

Enough. That's enough.

Ra laughed. He stood exactly where she had left him, holding her bracelet up toward the light of a streetlamp.

"If you give up this charade now, I'll let you li–"

Ravenna pulled the trigger, and her plasma bolt sank into Ra's abdomen.

"Not your call," she said flatly.

Ra frowned, looking downward. Blood spilled from his stomach onto the sidewalk.

Without hesitation, Ravenna walked toward him, firing one shot after the next. If he was an android, she knew one shot would not be sufficient.

An angry shout worked its way from Ra's throat as he launched himself toward her. Closing her eyes and bracing herself for the worst, she fired again.

Endless moments passed in an empty silence.

Ravenna forced her eyes open and let out a sharp breath. Ra lay at her feet, unmoving, a few of the bracelet's links spilling between his fingers and synthetic blood pooling in the new hole in his chest.

A scream cut through the night, followed by a succession of footsteps from the way the tourists had disappeared.

"Jo, call the police!" shouted a voice that sounded like the boy who'd walked past Ravenna's hiding place.

"Time's up," Ravenna breathed.

She turned on her heel and ran.

***

Clarisse surveyed Ra's unblinking emerald eyes. She'd always been unsettled by how inhuman they looked in each of the Seven.

Why couldn't our engineers at least try to make them pass for normal?

She sighed and pulled the white sheet covering the lower half of Ra's body up to conceal his face, as well.

"As promised," said Isabella's voice from behind her, "I will ensure that no one is looking for Ravenna."

Clarisse turned away from the dead android and faced Isabella, who stood in the chrome-plated lab's doorway.

"Thank you, ma'am," Clarisse said quietly.

Isabella nodded. "And this was with him."

She reached out and dropped Ravenna's golden bracelet into Clarisse's hand.

She's fine. She succeeded, and she's fine.

Still, Clarisse's mouth went dry, and she slipped the bracelet into her pocket without a word.

BROKEN

July 26, 2232

Mia made her way to the parking lot and the small black car that waited for her. She slipped into the driver's seat and began to sift through her purse for her keys. Driving wasn't entirely necessary, as she could have run the distance between the warehouse and the hotel room she'd been renting without difficulty. But she was trying to blend in, and there was nothing normal about running ten-plus miles without so much as breaking a sweat, especially at the pace she knew she could reach.

Blending in. It's never going to be that simple, is it?

It wasn't that she didn't look human. To all outside appearances, she was a typical American woman in her mid-20s. She was thin at 5'9", with brown eyes and sharp facial features. She didn't look out of the ordinary, but the fact that she'd technically never been born kept her from holding a legitimate driver's license. It and the rest of her personal documents had been forged to avoid drawing unwanted attention.

She withdrew her keys and wallet from her purse,

opening the wallet and glancing at the fake driver's license within.

Mia Warren.

Mia closed the wallet and replaced it in her purse, inserting her key into the ignition and starting the car. She pulled out of the parking lot and onto Park Avenue. Her car propelled itself upward automatically to fill the vacant space in the third tier of traffic, and she mentally cursed the buzzing, honking cluster that always filled Manhattan's streets.

After this, all I have left to do is wipe the LDE files. Shouldn't be that hard. Might as well check on him…

She turned right onto Gramercy Park South and followed it to its intersection with Irving and the large brick house that belonged to Eddie. She knew he had his father's luck in striking oil, which had all but vanished a century earlier, to thank for such a large property within the city's boundaries, and she couldn't rid her mind of the image of herself standing beside Eddie on that spotless, green lawn.

"Soon," she muttered with a tight shake of her head.

***

April 2223

Eddie drummed his fingers against the table in front of him. He fought the itch at the back of his mind telling him to glance over his shoulder and kept his eyes focused on the empty booth in front of him. He'd been given no details about whomever he was supposed to be meeting, and the longer he spent in the café, the more certain he became that he had been deceived.

In his periphery, he saw the middle-aged brunette from the table to his right stand and approach him. He pulled in a breath and rolled his shoulders backward.

She slipped into the bench opposite him, and he took

in her navy suit jacket and the determined set of her lips.

"Mr. Dodson." She inclined her head to him.

Eddie blinked. "You know my name, but I don't know yours. That's hardly fair."

She nodded and extended a hand. "You have a point. I'm Clarisse."

Eddie hesitated for the span of a heartbeat and then shook her hand.

"Not to be rude, Clarisse," he said, "but what is it exactly that you want from me?"

"Down to business already? All right." She shrugged. "I'd like to start by saying that it's not me that wants anything from you. It's the organization I work for. We've been watching you for quite some time now," Clarisse continued, "and we've come to learn a few things about you."

Eddie attempted to keep his tone devoid of emotion, though his discomfort was growing with each word she spoke. "Such as?"

"You're always doing everything you can to prove yourself, be it to your business partners, their family, or anyone else."

He said nothing. He felt no obligation to confirm something she'd evidently gathered by spying on him.

"Each of the LDE founders brings something different to the table. Damian Lawrence is the visionary, while Derek's more practical. And you're the real technical genius."

"Does any of this have a point?" The longer Eddie sat with Clarisse, the more he wished to get away from her.

"Yes, it does. Because we also know that you tend to go out of your way to help people. We need your help."

"With what?"

She took a deep breath. "As you may have heard, the army is in a bit of a bad spot, at the moment."

Eddie's stomach turned.

"A few years ago, they decided that the reason for their

failure was simple: soldiers are human."

Eddie raised an eyebrow. "Yes, they are."

"That's where my organization comes in. We reasoned that, without the possibility of human error, our armed forces would have a much better chance at holding their own against their enemies. Picture this: what if we didn't send human soldiers into battle? What if, instead, we sent—?"

"Androids."

She can't be serious, Eddie thought. *LDE doesn't build soldiers.*

"Exactly." Clarisse nodded.

"But... why come to me? Doesn't the government have anyone capable of doing this?"

Clarisse closed her eyes. "We thought so, once. During the last conflict in the Middle East, we assembled a group of people consisting of some of the greatest minds in the nation. We had the goal of creating the perfect soldier, and at one point, we thought we'd succeeded. We wanted the androids to be able to work effectively in all situations and without emotions disrupting the execution of their orders. Unfortunately, our plans worked too well. The androids did what they were supposed to; they took out a small group of enemy forces." She opened her eyes but did not look at Eddie. Instead, she folded her hands on the table and stared down at them. "But they didn't stop there. Apparently, a member of the enemy group escaped to a nearby town, and the androids followed him. They... they destroyed the entire town and everyone in it."

Eddie lowered his hands to rest on his knees beneath the table to keep Clarisse from seeing them tighten into fists. He'd never heard of such an atrocity being committed by androids. Try as he might, he could never imagine Lila, his company's first creation, doing something that heartless. But Clarisse had said that the military androids had been designed to act without emotion, and Eddie surmised that this was what separated them from his own creations. Lawrence-Dodson Enterprises thrived on being the only company that had mastered the near-human android.

Clarisse shook her head. "That was a long time ago. The fighting eventually ended, and... that was that. We didn't know what to do next. Without the pressure of an ongoing conflict, we didn't feel the need to give ourselves a time limit to perfect the process of creating the soldiers. We kept trying, testing our creations on a much smaller scale than before. They just... never seemed to work quite right. There was always a flaw. What that flaw was varied from one attempt to the next. The complete lack of morals, a physical problem like succumbing too easily to enemy fire, or any number of other things... we just couldn't get it right. But because it was a time of peace, we weren't too concerned. But now, with what's going on in Asia..."

"You're going to try again."

"Yes. But we've lost what little faith we had in the team that was supposed to be in charge of creating the soldiers." She took a deep breath. "You have no idea how long we've been watching you, and the others. In my personal opinion, if anyone can do this, it's you."

Clarisse rose from her seat.

"Thank you for your time, Mr. Dodson. I'll be in touch." Without another word, she departed.

Eddie laid his elbow on the table and dropped his face into his hand. "This is ludicrous," he mumbled.

Nevertheless, he was intrigued.

***

July 26, 2232

Mia drove past Eddie's home and toward the hotel. A few minutes later, she pulled into another parking lot and turned off the car. She took a deep breath and opened the glove compartment, reaching inside and removing the holofiles she'd stolen from Eddie's office at LDE. After she'd slipped the files safely into her purse, she opened the door, stepped out onto the pavement, and locked the car.

I can't believe I'm not more upset about this, she thought idly as she made her way toward the hotel.

The large front doors swung open at Mia's unspoken request, and she entered the lobby. She paid little attention to the smiling faces of the workers, to the smell of freshly ground coffee wafting from a machine in the corner, or to the other guests milling about. Instead she ignored it all and proceeded across the lobby, down the adjacent hallway, and into an elevator.

This part is almost over, she told herself as the elevator began to ascend. She felt a twinge of an emotion that she couldn't quite identify at this thought. It was foreign to her, this feeling brought on by the knowledge that she was about to terminate all evidence of the way she had come into existence. Though she would never know for certain if it was at all similar, she likened it somewhat to a human feeding her birth certificate to a paper shredder.

A paper shredder, she thought. *Wouldn't that be easier?*

But no. She knew what she had to do, and it was much more drastic than a paper shredder.

The elevator dinged, and the doors slid open. Mia stepped out into the hallway and turned left, reflexively following the path that led to room 407. This path was one that she had learned well over the past few weeks. She withdrew her keycard from her purse and scanned it through the panel beside the door.

"Welcome, Miss Warren."

Mia gave a hollow laugh at the automatic greeting and entered her room.

***

June 2224

Eddie threw open the door of the base and darted outside into the blinding sunlight. He scanned his surroundings frantically for the source of the crash he'd heard from within the building. His heart thumped so rapidly it nauseated him, and he couldn't rid himself of the flashes of Mia snapping the assault rifles of the soldiers tasked with testing her abilities. An image of her snapping the arm of one of the men turned Eddie's blood cold.

I don't know what I expected, but I wasn't ready for this.

Damian and Derek hadn't wanted their work weaponized. Eddie had hoped that Mia could be used to save the lives of soldiers, but now, he had no idea of what she was capable.

Two blocks down the road, a crowd was gathering—around what, Eddie couldn't tell. A police car had already arrived, and multiple other vehicles had ceased to move on the ground level of traffic while the cars flying above it continued onward. Eddie strained his eyes in an attempt to see what was happening.

"I didn't mean for it to turn out like this."

Eddie jumped. He turned to see Mia standing behind him. Her cropped auburn hair fell to her chin, and hesitation lurked in her eyes. Otherwise, her face was expressionless, but there was a strange quality in her voice that he did not recognize. It unnerved him.

What has she done?

"What are you talking about?"

"I never should have run. It was a mistake."

"Mia, what happened?" demanded Eddie.

She opened her mouth as though to speak and then shut it again. She turned and strode off down the street and away from the gathering mass of people.

"Mia!"

She continued to walk away. Eddie hesitated, torn by the obligation to follow her and the desire to see for himself what she was avoiding. He cursed under his breath and started toward the expanding crowd.

By the time he reached the scene, two more police cars had arrived along with an ambulance. Silently, he wove his way through the crowd, attempting to piece together a rough interpretation of what had happened.

"Reckless driving..."

"...wasn't paying attention..."

"...can't believe the idiocy..."

"Someone ran in front of me!" exclaimed a man in a red jacket. He spoke frantically to one of the police officers and a gaggle of eavesdroppers. Eddie pretended not to be listening as he passed them. "I swerved—I didn't want to hit her, officer—and—and—I hit them! I didn't mean to, I swear! It wasn't my fault!"

Eddie's breath swept from his lungs as he caught sight of the accident.

A van was embedded in the side of a small black car. The latter was reduced to a nearly unrecognizable heap of metal. It lay upside-down, and both front doors had been removed. No one was inside.

EMTs were lifting two stretchers into the ambulance. The person on each was covered with a white blanket from head to toe. After the ambulance had been loaded, two of the EMTs shut the doors and climbed into the vehicle.

"Did they make it out all right?" Eddie asked one of the uniformed medics who remained. He already knew the answer, but he could not process it. If Mia was responsible for this, he couldn't allow himself to believe people had died because of her. This wasn't combat. These people hadn't been soldiers.

The EMT turned to him and shook her head sadly. "The media's going to have a field day."

"I'm sorry," Eddie breathed.

A hand gripped his shoulder.

"We need to go," said Mia's voice in his ear.

"Did you run in front of that van?" Eddie hissed, his

voice too low for the EMT to hear.

"Come on. We need to get out of–"

"Who were they?" Eddie asked the EMT, ignoring Mia entirely.

The woman sighed as she climbed into the front seat of the ambulance. She called to Eddie over her shoulder. "Senator Henry Lawrence and his wife."

And the world was spinning. Eddie couldn't breathe.

This isn't happening.

He backed up slowly, his mind reeling as he stepped off the road and began retracing his steps toward West Point, Mia keeping pace at his side.

No. This isn't possible. They weren't supposed to be here. They were supposed to be back in New York.

A glance back to the scene of the accident told him that the media had arrived. News vans and paparazzi swarmed the demolished car. Eddie tuned them out. He didn't need to know anything more. It had happened, and it was his fault.

Damian and Derek will never forgive me. And Desdemona...

"Eddie, I–"

"Don't." He turned to face Mia, staring at her coldly. "Don't even try."

He did not know what he would do with her, now. He couldn't stand to look at her for more than a moment, and he averted his eyes to the ground at her feet. Eddie took a deep breath.

"Come on," he said. "We were never here."

And you never existed.

***

July 26, 2232

Mia surveyed the window that would look out onto the street below, were the heavily embroidered ivory curtains not drawn to shut out the light from outside. She eyed the small collection of books that lay spread out on the table, some with dog-eared pages saving the place of the woman who couldn't seem to focus on one of them for an extended period of time. She glanced at the bed and the unmade blankets that matched the curtains.

And the fireplace.

Mia moved to stand beside it, rummaging through her purse until she was absolutely certain that she had collected every last file from it. She then flipped the switch on the wall beside the hearth, and the logs ignited with a burst of flame and bathed the room in flickering light.

Mia tossed the holofiles onto the fire, watching as the flames licked at them. Tearing her eyes away from the sight, Mia surveyed the room again. The curtains, which would keep the outside world from seeing what she was about to do. The books, which had to be considered acceptable losses. Replaceable. The bed, which was one of only a few reminders that she had slept here. That she lived here.

That she lived at all, if that was indeed what she did.

***

June 2224

Eddie stared unblinkingly at the perfect replica of himself.

This is wrong.

He examined the short, dark hair and grey eyes he'd seen in the mirror all his life as they were now reflected back at him in the form of the android copy he'd agreed to allow.

Eddie remembered the moment that Damian, turned away to stare out the window of his office with his hands braced on the sill, had suggested they use their work to find a way to preserve human life after death. Consumed by guilt for the part he'd played in the death of Damian and Derek's parents, Eddie had allowed himself to be the test subject. He'd allowed the invasive procedure to copy his memories, his mannerisms, his entire personality into this duplicate body.

I want it decommissioned and hidden in the warehouse. I don't want anyone to know we did this.

If the experiment could keep someone from losing all of a loved one to death, he'd believed it was worth it.

As the duplicate blinked and pulled in a breath, Eddie questioned whether that was true.

***

July 26, 2232

Mia moved in a flash to the table and picked up the paperback copy of *A Separate Peace* she'd left face down on it. She was fond of this volume, but she could buy another copy. There were few things in her life that weren't disposable.

She returned to the fireplace and watched the files burn. As each was destroyed, it projected its contents randomly into the air. Fragments of sentences overlapped as the files attempted to make known the information they held for the final time.

"…is extremely dangerous…" "…deactivated after the incident at West Point…" "…will serve as the replacement for human soldiers…" "…responsible for the deaths of Henry and Samantha Lawrence in June of 2224…" "…no emotional inhibitions…" "…does not hesitate to kill…"

Mia had seen enough.

After a few moments, the last of the files had dissolved into ash. Mia held the copy of *A Separate Peace* out toward the fireplace and took a few steps forward. She held the book over the flames until the top right corner sparked and the fire began to blacken it. She then threw the book across the room, and it fell to the ground at the hem of the curtains.

***

July 24, 2232

Eddie watched her as she descended the steps of the police station. Her dark-blond hair was a bit disheveled as it fell in waves past her shoulders, and her eyes were ringed with dark circles. Still, Desi was just as beautiful as she'd always been.

Eddie remembered how peaceful she'd looked when he'd awoken in the middle of the night to see her sleeping beside him. He'd tucked a lock of hair behind her ear to give him a better view of her face and watched her until he'd fallen asleep again.

When he'd awoken the next morning, she'd been gone.

Eddie smiled slightly and pushed off of the car he'd been leaning against to open the passenger door for her. A light blush tinted her cheeks, and she brushed past him silently to climb into the car.

He rolled his shoulders backward and closed the door before sliding into his seat and starting the car. He turned to study her, and he found her eyes closed. He returned his focus to the road and spurred the car forward.

"Are you all right?" he asked as he drove. He tried to keep his mind on the vehicles surrounding him, but he found it hard to think about anything but Desi.

"Were my brothers too busy to bail me out themselves?" she asked.

"Damian's still out of town until tomorrow, and Derek won't be back until the day after."

She sighed heavily, and he glanced toward her, his heart leaping into his throat at the sight of the blue eyes he'd come to adore. When she turned away to stare out the window, he felt as though the floor of the car had dropped out from under him to leave him to the road below.

"Sorry to disappoint you," he muttered.

"No, I appreciate you coming to get me. Thank you."

A pause followed, and the only sound was that of the outside traffic.

"Desi, I have told you that I'm here if you need to talk, haven't I? About absolutely anything?"

"Appreciate it. And Desdemona, please."

"Desdemona," he repeated with a sigh. "Yes, of course."

I suppose it doesn't matter what's happened between us, does it?

Eddie nearly forgot to turn on the blinker before following a large white truck around the corner onto Amsterdam Avenue. A sedan sped past them on the layer of traffic hovering above Eddie's car, and he briefly debated turning on the radio to alleviate the tension.

"How mad is Damian?" Desi asked.

Eddie shrugged. "He didn't say. Honestly, I think he's more worried about you than anything."

Desi sighed, drumming her fingertips against the console between the seats. "I'm fine."

He glanced toward her, and she met his eyes for a moment before looking away, directing her attention out the windshield.

"I didn't actually do anything illegal," she continued, apparently hoping this was slightly more convincing than her last statement. "Marley was the one who was going to try to drive, and her boyfriend tripped into the table. I offered to pay for it, but–"

"Drunk and disorderly conduct. That's what they're charging you with. Desdemona, I can smell the alcohol on you from here."

She sighed, tipping her head back to stare at the roof of the car as she blinked back tears. "I don't know what I'm doing," she muttered. Several seconds passed in silence before Eddie spoke softly.

"What do you mean? Now, or in general?"

"Either. I–I don't know. Damian and Derek both have everything figured out. They've been working on the damned company since they were in high school, and you've been right there with them, all of you completely sure what you want out of life and how to get it. And what did I do? I studied four years of theater and haven't even been to an audition in months, and what the hell did those robotics classes do for me? You can't honestly tell me the three of you would even think about hiring me. And Damian always has this—this *disappointment* in his eyes when he looks at me, and I can't handle it. He's got everything he's always wanted, and what do I have?"

Me. If you'll just see that.

She watched him for a moment, exasperation in the set of her lips and regret in her eyes.

"Please don't tell him I said anything," she implored, her voice cracking on the last word.

Eddie reached out to rest his hand on hers, and relief swept over him when she did not draw back from the touch.

"I won't," he said. "You have my word."

She nodded stiffly and turned away to stare out the window once again. Eddie's heart raced, and the words burst from his lips before he could stop them.

"Desdemona… can we please talk about—"

"We can't."

***

July 26, 2232

As Mia watched, the fire began to spread up the embroidered ivory material. The flames leapt around the room, beginning to engulf it.

"I think it's time to check out."

Mia turned on her heel and opened the door, closing it briskly behind her as she started swiftly down the hallway.

The elevator no longer awaited her. Mia pressed the down button and glanced up at the lights above the golden doors, which told her the elevator was on its way up from the lobby. She tapped her left foot impatiently. There were other ways out of the building, but this was the least conspicuous.

Humans are too lazy for the stairs unless they know something's wrong.

The doors dinged and opened at last, and a man in a white button-down shirt stepped out. He smiled at her as they switched places, a gesture which she returned as she pressed the button for the first floor.

His smile faded as abruptly as it had appeared. "Do you smell smoke?" he asked.

Mia took a deep breath, pulling in the charred smell that now filled the hallway.

"Yeah, I do."

The man's expression of alarm disappeared behind the elevator doors, and Mia moved downward toward the lobby.

***

July 25, 2232

Eddie heaved a sigh and stared at the holographic readout in front of him without seeing a single projected word.

He hated that no matter how he tried, he couldn't stop thinking about her. Her beautiful blue eyes, her bright smile, the perfect softness of her lips against his, the warmth of her skin…

Stop it, he ordered himself. *Now.*

He closed his eyes and lowered his head into his hand.

What good will it do? She doesn't love you.

For a moment, it had seemed as though she'd loved him. She'd let him see her in a way he liked to think no one else had. Desi had always been private about her innermost emotions, and even if it had been a momentary lapse in judgment on her part, she had confided in him about her parents' deaths.

She wouldn't have, if she'd known they were your fault.

His jaw tightened. He'd wanted to tell her for years how much she meant to him, how much he cared for her. He'd finally found a way to show her, and if only for a moment, she'd shown him something similar. Or perhaps she'd just wanted the night of comfort and the illusion of reciprocated feelings. Perhaps she hadn't actually cared for him or expected him to truly care for her at all.

She wouldn't use you that way.

Eddie was certain the feeling of nausea that had settled in the pit of his stomach was a permanent one. He'd been unable to escape it since the morning Desi had left his bedroom with an apologetic glance and a few words about how they couldn't sleep together again.

He couldn't let her go that easily. He cared too much—he loved her too much.

"I have to do right by you," he muttered.

Eddie let the holofile fall from his grasp, and it clanged against the shining metal surface of his desk. He pushed his chair backward and slid to his feet, his jaw set, and his eyes fixed on the panel set into the wall opposite him. Within a few strides, he had reached the panel, and he pressed his palm to the scanner.

"Welcome, Eddie."

He said nothing in reply to the machine's automated female voice; he focused his thoughts on pulling forth the proper model from the storage vaults in the warehouse's unmapped depths. Since LDE's creation, Eddie had been able to access and store any prototype he was so inclined to attempt, as had Derek and Damian. Eddie had no idea what the others might have stored within the warehouse, and the knowledge that they could not access his private experiments had helped him to sleep on several tortured nights.

I can't give your parents back to you, he thought, only half-wishing Desi could hear him, *but I can start to pay for what I've done.*

He concentrated on using the warehouse's neural interface to bring Mia from her place in the basement level of the warehouse's storage area. Within moments, the silver doors set into the wall just to the left of where Eddie stood cracked open, and the familiar metallic pod pushed through the opening.

The *whoosh-hiss* of decompression broke the silence pressing in on Eddie. He watched as the pod's glass lid defogged and the figure within became clearer.

"It's my fault," Eddie breathed. "But I will do everything I can to fix it."

***

July 25, 2232

Mia tightened her grip on Eddie's throat. The mechanical heart he'd placed in her chest was close to thrumming its way out of her, and for the first time in her life, she felt true regret. She didn't want to hurt him.

"You want to shut me down? For *her*?" she snapped.

Eddie pulled at Mia's fingers, working unsuccessfully to pry them from his neck.

"You–are–dangerous," he choked.

"Whose fault is that?" she cried.

Her arm trembled as she held him off the ground, and she briefly wondered whether she'd been built with the capacity to shed tears.

"I'm what you made me," she continued. "And you're supposed to love me."

Eddie's lips moved once more, but no sound left them. His grey eyes fluttered shut.

Mia glanced to the cryogenic tube she'd been trapped inside for the better part of eight years. She loosened her grip and began to lower Eddie to the floor.

"Maybe the other you will," she whispered.

LILA

"Hey, watch it! What do you think you're doing?"

"Sorry." The young woman averted her eyes from the man she had inadvertently run into on the crowded New York street. She hadn't been paying attention to where she was walking, and she knew the scuffle was her fault.

That was the only thing she knew.

She looked up at the pastel clouds as the sun fell over the skyline, and she let out a long sigh. The emptiness bothered her the most. The space in her mind where her memories should be, which was now an endless blank canvas protected by an impenetrable wall. The more she focused on remembering, the greater the strain became. It was as though something was deliberately keeping her out of her own past, which infuriated her. Before walking through downtown Manhattan in the early hours of that July morning, she had no idea what she had done or who she was, apart from what she had learned from the silver bracelet dangling from her right wrist.

The engraved plate between the bracelet's small central links read "LILA."

Apart from what must be her name, she had only one clue to the truth about her life: a deep, unshakable need to leave New York. Lila couldn't explain why she felt so strongly that she had to get out of the city—she only knew that the thought of staying longer than necessary chilled her on some deep, fundamental level.

"Hey, sweetheart."

The voice had come from her right, from down an alleyway shadowed by towering buildings and untouched by street lamps. Lila didn't look for the speaker, nor did she react. She continued to walk. After several seconds, it became obvious that she was being followed. She felt a presence close enough behind her to be unsettling but not enough to draw the attention of passersby.

"Where are you headed?"

"That's none of your concern. I'm going there alone."

Lila tuned in to the people around her, and she felt that more than one of them was on her trail. Still, she didn't look at them. Her heart rate and pace remained even, and she wasn't the least bit afraid, though rationally she believed she should be. Whoever she really was, she realized that she had, at least, not been a coward.

Someone laughed; the voice was different, this time. "Alone? Why would a pretty girl like you be all alone on a night like this?"

She tensed instinctively as a hand grabbed her shoulder, and at this, she stopped walking.

"Don't touch me."

There was another laugh from behind her. "Why not? Gonna do something about it? You look like you've got money, sweetheart. Let's have a look at you."

A second hand grabbed her, followed by a third. The first still had a tight grip on her shoulder, and the others restrained her arms. As one, they pulled her roughly backward.

Lila reacted on reflex.

She pulled her right arm free and, in one fluid motion, formed a fist and sank it into the gut of the man restraining her left arm. In the same movement, she kicked back with her left leg, knocking someone else's feet out from under him. She grabbed the arm of another, holding it with one hand and bringing the other down on it swiftly. Beneath her hands, she heard a sickening snap. The man cried out in pain. He exchanged an incredulous glance with another from his group.

Someone grabbed her left arm again. She reached behind her without looking to see which of the men it was and pulled him forward, ducking as he flew over her head and landed on the street, his arm bending unnaturally beneath him.

Now, terror was etched into each of their faces. Two of them bent down to help their fallen counterpart stand, pulling him to his feet and supporting him. Then they all ran, scattering like roaches as they fled. She counted them in their retreat, and she saw that she had fought off five assailants. She turned away and continued walking.

They were terrified of me, Lila thought. She bit her lip and replayed the scene in her mind, and she realized just how unlikely it was for her to have been able to defend herself so skillfully against so many people. *I think I'm terrified of myself.*

She shook her head, positively clueless about what to do next. More than anything else, she needed privacy and a place to think, to collect herself and evaluate her predicament. She looked up and scanned the street, and her eyes fell on a large hotel a few buildings away. If nothing else, she could find a place to sit in the lobby until she had made a greater decision on what to do with herself.

Lila reached the building and passed through the sliding glass doors that automatically allowed her entrance. Her eyes adjusted rapidly to the artificial lights, and she took in her surroundings. Pristine white chairs and chaises lined the walls, and three silver chandeliers hung from the arched ceiling. A receptionist with her hair pulled back into a tight bun smiled and waved to Lila from the desk at the opposite end of the long room.

This place felt startlingly familiar.

Lila looked down into the marble floor, and she saw her reflection. Her roadside brawl had left no evidence; her blond hair had fallen perfectly around her face once more—her face, which had not flushed a bit from the effort.

She started for one of the chaises, planning to rest for a few minutes and devise a plan, but the receptionist beckoned to her. Confused, she crossed the lobby to the desk where the woman sat, still smiling.

"Welcome back, ma'am. We have your room ready."

Lila blinked. *Maybe if I just play along*, she thought, *I'll figure it out.*

"Yes, thank you," she said, forcing herself to return the receptionist's smile with one she hoped was convincing enough.

The woman nodded. "I'll show you to it, myself. Right this way, please." She removed a key card from behind the desk, stood, and motioned for Lila to follow her as she walked toward a door behind her and to the left.

Thoroughly lost but feigning control of the situation, Lila followed as the receptionist led her down a spotless white hallway and to an elevator at the other end. The ride was a silent one. A million questions buzzed through Lila's mind, but something within her stopped her from asking them. She had a strange feeling that it was not the right time, and when she had so little else at her disposal, she believed she should trust her intuition.

The pair left the elevator on the fifteenth floor, and Lila followed the receptionist to a door on the opposite side of the hallway. The receptionist swiped the key card she held, and when the lock clicked, she motioned to the door and smiled brightly. Lila found the other woman's perpetually-sunny demeanor a bit grating, but she said nothing. Frowning slightly, Lila turned the glass doorknob and stepped into the room.

Her jaw dropped. She stood at the entrance to a suite,

and the furniture was extravagant and made of white, polished wood. On the opposite wall, the fading sunlight of dusk streamed in the glass balcony door. In the muted reddish light, the golden satin bedclothes shimmered.

Lila stood perfectly still, astounded.

"Will that be all, ma'am?"

Lila nodded. "Yes, thank you very much." The receptionist—Lila noticed for the first time that the woman was wearing a nametag that identified her as Danielle—turned and walked back down the hall. Lila entered the room, closing the door behind her. She crept toward the bed, incredibly uneasy, and sat on the edge.

Okay, she knew me, she thought. *That's several steps ahead of where I am, right now. But why did I get the vibe that I can't trust her? It's so strange.*

Lila shook her head, leaning backward. She would have time to think when she woke. She hadn't slept in… frankly, she had no idea how long. The first thing she remembered was walking the city's streets before dawn had broken. How she had ended up there remained unclear, as did why, and in the intervening hours, she'd been unable to learn anything apart from what was probably her name.

Sleep did not elude her, as she had feared it would. In a matter of moments, her mind had drifted far away from the hotel and into comfortable blackness.

***

Lila jumped, startled by the abrupt change of scenery. She was no longer in her hotel room; instead, she stood in a lab plated in chrome panels. Though she could not recall ever being here before, the room felt glaringly familiar.

She wasn't alone. On her left stood a man with his back to her. The more she tried to concentrate on what he looked like, the more her head ached. He was an indistinct blur, his true nature indiscernible.

Lila abandoned the pursuit of the man's identity and directed her attention instead to the one standing to her right. Unlike the first, he was incredibly clear to her. His hair was light brown, and his brown eyes were locked on hers. He was speaking to her—pleading with her. She shook her head. She couldn't hear what he was saying, couldn't hear anything at all. Her ears were filled with deafening silence.

Suddenly, the scene changed. Lila stood now in a lobby very slightly reminiscent of the hotel's. It had a high ceiling and a chrome desk, but this room was far more business-like than the one several floors below where she slept. She stood about ten feet from a row of glass doors, looking down at a figure that was slouched against the one farthest to her left.

It was the man from the lab; the one who had stood on her right, begging her for something, to do—or not to do—something. But what?

For the first time, she looked down at her own hand. She was holding a plasma gun.

Why? Where had she found it? She hadn't been holding it in the lab. Or had she? How had she gotten here, to the lobby?

Only a second had passed.

The man spoke. This time, all she could hear was his voice—no background noise or abrasive silence.

"You don't have to do this, Lila," he said. "You don't have to—" He glanced over her shoulder, seeming to rethink the statement he had been about to make. "Just remember who you are. Remember who I—"

And she was in her hotel room, her head spinning with the sound that had launched her out of the dream as abruptly as she had entered it.

A gunshot.

***

Lila stared into the bathroom mirror at her tearstained face. Her eyes stung, and her hair stuck out at odd angles.

She didn't care. She had no self-pity. Though she was alone in a hotel in a city she couldn't remember after dreaming about someone she didn't know, it wasn't herself she cried for. It was the man from her dream.

He had seemed so real to her, as had the pain in his eyes as he implored her not to... but she couldn't have really done it. There was no way she could have killed someone. After all, not all dreams held significance. She could've seen a story on the news the day before that had disturbed her or paid too much attention at the press conference she had stumbled upon as she'd tried to leave Manhattan, and the dream could've been her coping mechanism.

What was that robotics engineer's name who was killed? Lawrence?

But she knew she was deluding herself. The images had been far too clear to have been concocted by her weary mind. She had known this man. What remained to be seen was how, and what had happened to him.

She slid open a drawer beneath the sink and withdrew a silver hairbrush. She ran it distractedly through her golden locks as she tried to remember.

"You don't have to do this, Lila," the man in her dream had said.

He'd known her name. That was something, at least. The way he'd spoken to her... they had been more than acquaintances. But something he'd said continued to trouble her.

"Just remember who you are. Remember who I—"

Who he what? Lila sighed. *I need answers.*

She left the brush on the sink and stepped back into her room. She hadn't needed to make the bed; she hadn't pulled back the covers the previous night, nor had she displaced them while she slept. Though she had expected such a disturbing dream to cause her to toss and turn, it hadn't. The projection emitted by the clock on her nightstand told her it was 4:37 in the afternoon, and she couldn't imagine how she had been exhausted enough to sleep for so long.

Lila moved to the door. She took a deep breath and turned the glass knob, stepping into the hall. Retracing the steps she had taken upon her arrival, she found the elevator and rode it to the lobby. Danielle the receptionist waved as she passed, and Lila returned the wave with a forced smile.

As Lila moved through the lobby, her shoes clicked on the floor. The other guests, most of them loitering near the walls with no apparent purpose, watched her as she passed. She kept her eyes fixed ahead of her, and soon she was pushing open the large double-doors at the head of the room. She stepped out into the summer heat, wishing for a change of clothing, or at least for some small amount of money. She had not yet been asked to pay for her room, and she was yet to understand why.

She wasn't entirely certain where she was headed, now. Her restlessness demanded she leave the hotel, but her lack of money limited her options. She caught sight of a restaurant down the street and started toward it through the mid-afternoon throng, thinking that even if she couldn't order, she could hide indoors from the heat until she could form a better plan.

Lila let out a sharp breath as a dark-haired woman bumped hard into her shoulder. The woman muttered an apology, which Lila returned on reflex, glancing toward her.

An image shot through Lila's mind of someone with the same pale face, the same hazel eyes and dark hair as the woman beside her, though in that image, she was several years younger.

Startled by this flash of memory, Lila hurried onward, closing the distance rapidly between herself and the restaurant. She'd made it a few yards when a whistle demanded her attention. Her mind screamed at her to keep walking, to get away. However, the idea that she'd actually *recognized* that woman was more than she'd had moments ago, and it was enough to convince her to turn around.

As she'd expected, the brunette was watching her from where she now stood on the other side of the street, lips curled into a smirk.

"*Lila*," she mouthed.

At the same moment the woman started forward, pushing her way through a crowd of people gathered on the sidewalk, Lila turned back in the direction of her hotel and moved toward it at a run.

Something whispered from the back of Lila's mind that she could outrun the other woman easily—that if she ran far enough and fast enough, she would lose her pursuer. She could escape. But only for now. As strange as this feeling was, even stranger was the certainty with which she knew that the victory of escape would be fleeting. That she would not be free for long. That the woman she'd seen would never stop hunting her.

Perhaps Lila was beginning to remember. She knew enough, she reasoned, to protect herself, but not enough to understand why this person posed such a threat to her in the first place.

Lila flew into the hotel and moved as quickly as she could to her room. She swiped her card and wrenched back the door, slamming and locking it behind her after she entered. She proceeded to her bathroom, shutting and locking this second door for good measure.

Her breathing quick and shallow, Lila threw her back against the wall, closing her eyes through the pain as she sank to the floor. She pulled her knees up and rested her head on them, biting her lip.

What am I going to do? I have to find out what happened to me. I need to know who that man was in my dream. I need to know why this woman is following me. What did I do to her? What did I do to—to him?

She ordered herself to hold still and bring her emotions into check. She forced one deep breath after the other into her lungs and out again, and soon, she lost track of how long she had been sitting still. With a sigh, she forced a blend of anger, despair, and frustration from her lips and pushed herself to her feet. She unlocked and opened the door, beginning to cross her room to the pair made of sliding glass that let out onto the balcony.

Suddenly, she heard movement outside in the corridor, and she froze. A shadow played on the carpet beneath the door, accompanied by the pressing of buttons on a keypad. If someone knew the code to Lila's room, she knew, they could have entered at any time without the use of her card—not only while she was outside, but while she slept. She would've never been safe.

As her heart pounded, Lila crossed the room to the back door, turning off the lights at the switch near the exit. Lila opened the door onto the balcony and slipped outside as it closed automatically behind her.

She surveyed her surroundings. She'd spent longer than she'd realized in the bathroom; night had fallen. There was no easy way to the ground. She leaned over the railing, searching manically for options. The highway below was backed up with traffic. Hovercars, hovercycles, and pedestrians stretched as far as the eye could see.

She heard the scanner beep somewhere behind her. Her breath caught in her throat as she realized how little time she had. Concealed by the wall separating the balcony from the connected room, Lila was invisible to whoever was inside. But how long that would remain true was in question. The balcony, formerly shrouded in darkness, was now bathed in light. Lila's eyes widened in horror. *No...*

Footsteps signaled someone's approach. She couldn't allow herself to be captured. She had to be the one to discover what had happened to her. No one else would understand. Whatever she had done, she was sorry. Beyond all words, she was sorry. But she couldn't expect everyone to be so forgiving. Would they really believe her? She doubted it.

Jump. Jump, you'll be fine.

Lila edged to the side of the balcony farthest from the door.

That's insane. So why does it feel like the safest option?

Once more, she looked down. And, taking a deep, shaky breath, she threw herself over the edge.

As she hurtled downward, the world whipped around her, flying upward faster than Lila could blink. Falling end over end, she attempted to regain her composure well enough at least to see which way was down. The layers upon layers of hovercars rushed ominously ever nearer, and she knew it was only a matter of time before she made impact. Eventually, she managed to right herself, if only momentarily. She looked down and instinctively decided on a course of action. A dark green hovercar was approaching her at roughly the right speed to catch her.

Lila turned her body down once more and made a futile attempt to guide her flight pattern. She held her breath as the roar of the air rushing past her became nearly unbearable, counting down the seconds until her estimated contact. *Not long now... Five... Four... Three...*

At the last possible second, Lila turned to face the sky once more.

She landed with a crash on the roof of the car. As it sped on its course, Lila was thrown back, sliding the few feet to the car's rear, frantically searching for a place to grab on and finding nothing.

Her scream was lost in the night air as she flew off the back of the car.

The familiar sensation of being drowned in air overwhelmed her as she rushed downward for the second time. This had been a terrible decision. *No*, she corrected herself as she plummeted downward. *The worse choice would've been allowing myself to be captured.*

Regardless, there was no turning back, now.

A surge of pain spread through her as she collided with something. This time, the car stopped. Lila's back ached and her eyes closed as her head swam in the aftershock.

She barely registered the sound of a door opening.

"Are you okay, lady?" someone asked her.

"Hm...?" She found her focus slipping away.

The man who had spoken to her sighed in what sounded like frustration.

"You fell from the sky and landed on my car. Are you all right?"

Lila felt the shock of her impact wear off somewhat, and she forced her eyes open to find the man watching her closely. He was also standing on the ground, which meant Lila was done falling. *Oh, thank God.*

"I... yes, thank you." She attempted a feeble smile and pushed herself up onto her elbows.

"Are you sure you should be trying to get up? I mean, which floor did you fall from?" He looked up at the hotel's gleaming exterior. By this time, others had stopped their cars and were beginning to gather around Lila and the man.

She nodded feebly. "I'm fine, really." With a gulp, she pushed herself off the roof of the car. There was a general intake of breath around her as she rolled onto the pavement of the road below. The world seemed to spin again as she stood, and a relieved sigh spread through the gathered crowd.

"Hey!" called someone from her left. "I know you!"

Lila tensed. "I... I don't really re–"

Someone else gasped.

"That's–she's–Lila! Someone call the police!"

A murmur spread through the crowd, rapidly growing into a din.

No... Not now. Not... everyone!

She turned and ran, without another word, for the sidewalk on the opposite side of street from the hotel. They were shouting, now, calling incomprehensible things after her as she pushed her way out of the cloud of people. Her breathing quick and shallow, she flew down the street and around the corner.

As she ran, the pieces began to click into place in her distraught mind. She was running at much too rapid a pace to be considered normal, and not a bead of sweat had begun to form anywhere on her body. She was disoriented from her fall, but should she not be dead?

"What am I?" she breathed.

***

After what felt like hours of searching, she'd found a window small enough to slip into that led into the basement of an old, abandoned brick building. The darkness in which she now sat in the back corner was a considerable departure from the grandeur of her hotel room, but after the crowd's reaction to the sight of her, she didn't believe the public was the best place to be, at the moment.

She'd been sitting in silence for quite a while apart from her own ragged breath and the pounding of her heart in her ears when a voice reached her from up the ramp leading to the main level.

"Hello?"

Lila's eyes widened in terror. Was nowhere safe? She scooted backward, her back pressing hard against the wall as she willed herself to become invisible in the near-perfect darkness of the basement. A few moments later, a shape came into view: the figure of a man descending the ramp, holding what looked like a plasma gun, from what Lila could discern of the outline in the faint illumination that reached the man from the street lamps outside the windows.

"Hello?" the man asked again. Lila held perfectly still. "If you come out now, I promise I won't hurt you."

For an instant, she weighed her options. His words sounded sincere enough, but he was holding a gun, and she had no idea who he was or whether he was trustworthy. Still, he didn't appear to be leaving, and perhaps he would be less inclined to use force if she didn't provoke him. She pushed herself to her feet.

"Lila?" asked the man.

"Who—who are you?"

"What do you mean?"

"Who are you?" she repeated. She'd had enough of people knowing her while she knew nothing. She'd had enough of running without knowing why and questions without answers.

She watched the man's outline as he moved along the wall on the other side of the room, and then all at once, the basement was bathed in light. Aside from a few scattered boxes and stains along the concrete floor, Lila was alone with the newcomer. His features were sharp, his hair a sandy blond and his eyes blue. He was almost painfully familiar, his name on the tip of Lila's tongue, but she could not find it.

She took a step backward, the cool wall meeting her back as she glanced from the man's face to his gun and back.

"Lila? What are you doing down here?"

She briefly contemplated fabricating some sort of story to tell him, but she knew this would be futile. There was no use in lying when she had no idea what the truth was.

"I don't know where else to go," she said. "Who are you?"

He stared at her for a long moment, frowning, and she believed he was trying to determine whether she was serious.

"How can you not know me?" he asked, taking a step toward her. "It's me! It's Derek!"

"Derek who?" Lila's voice became more desperate with each word she spoke, and she felt as though she was losing her mind, reaching for memories that slipped through her fingers like water no matter how she struggled to pull them back.

"Derek Lawrence!" His voice was exasperated, and

though she couldn't blame him, his agitation served only to heighten hers. She shifted backward, pressing tighter against the wall behind her. He sighed and spoke again, his tone considerably softer, this time. "Don't you know me?"

She shook her head. "No. I–I don't remember anything before yesterday. The first thing I remember, I was walking around New York, seeing something about a *murder* at a press conference!" She froze as something clicked into place in her mind. "I think his name was Lawrence, too."

Derek flinched. "Damian?" he asked, his tone so flat she knew he must've been fighting to keep it that way.

Lila nodded. "I think so. And the hotel receptionist knew me–she said I had a room, but she didn't ask me to pay, and–" She struggled to sift through the mess of thoughts assaulting her mind with no idea where to begin. "–why do people know me while I have no idea who I am? Why do you know me? What about the woman with the dark hair, the one who looked at me like she wanted me dead? What about the people on the street?"

Her voice broke, and her eyes fell to the floor.

"I've known you all your life," said Derek after a moment. "The receptionist knew you because you live there, and if what you say about your memory is true, it's a miracle you ended up there to start with. The hotel called me after you got back today to let me know you were there before the police found you, and I've been looking for you. I want to give you a chance to prove you didn't do this, because I really don't want to believe you did."

The police? thought Lila. *Maybe things are as bad as I thought.*

"Why are the police looking for me?" she asked quietly.

"They think you killed Damian." Derek sighed, and there was a sadness in his eyes that pained Lila to watch. "My brother."

Lila felt as though the wind had been knocked from her lungs by force, and she struggled fruitlessly for her voice for several moments. Eventually, Derek spoke again.

"We have a security video that places you there, when it happened. I wanted to find you before we told anyone, but my business partner decided to tell the media, which is why everyone seems to know. And if someone was looking at you like she wanted you dead, I would imagine that's the assassin my sister hired, who is probably looking for you right now. Come on." He lowered the gun, and some of her tension vanished. An instant passed, and he extended his hand toward her.

If it's even a possibility that I was involved in his brother's death, thought Lila, *he has every reason to want to harm me, but he isn't. For some reason, he said he wants to believe I didn't do it. And I don't feel like I should be afraid of him. Honestly, what do I have to lose? What other option do I have?*

She took his hand, and he led her up the ramp and toward the building's exit. Lila followed Derek out onto the street and to his car, where he opened the passenger door for her. She climbed into the seat, and when he closed the door behind her, she caught sight of a few papers lying beside her feet. Upon closer inspection, she realized the paper on top was a blueprint. The image the paper bore was that of a woman—of *her.*

Her eyes widening, she shifted her focus to the text at the top of the page.

"Property of Lawrence-Dodson Enterprises. L.I.L.A.: Lawrences' Intelligent Living Android."

The driver's side door opened and Derek climbed into the car, shutting the door before starting the vehicle and spurring it forward.

"You don't have to be so tense, you know," he said. "I'm not going to hurt you. I… really don't think you could've done this. Not to Damian."

Lila barely heard his words. Her head was spinning as she understood why her fall from the fifteenth floor had left her without a scratch. Derek had known her for her entire life because he'd created her—he and his brother, presumably. The brother everyone but Derek believed Lila had murdered.

Perhaps, she surmised, her creators were exceptionally gifted. Perhaps they had made her intentionally as close to human as possible, to the point of fooling even herself. If so, she thought bitterly, they had certainly succeeded. Despite the strength she knew coursed through her with each movement she made, she felt less like an unstoppable force of mechanical genius and closer to a young woman stranded in a foreign place with no way to return home.

As she looked toward the man beside her, however, she thought that at least she now had someone on her side, someone who could help her begin to understand. For now, that was enough.

DIVISION

"This wasn't supposed to happen," said Rachel. "No one else was supposed to die." She stared down into her coffee cup and shook her head. Her shoulders were slumped, and she would not raise her eyes to meet Andrew's.

He knew she blamed herself. She always did, when something went wrong. He had tried time and again to convince her that the Division had been unable to be controlled completely since its creation. When so many independent variables were at play, the events the Division had been created to forestall had been, unfortunately, unstoppable.

This would've been true no matter how capable a leader was in charge, but on that point, Andrew had not yet managed to make Rachel see reason. He'd watched her put out fires since the day she'd taken over the organization that her mother had begun during Rachel's childhood. Andrew could not begin to understand how difficult it must've been to grow up with the pressures of being watched by the nation as Rachel had been.

He couldn't imagine it, but he tried.

He reached out and wrapped his hands around hers, and she looked at him at last. Her green eyes were pained, and the sight of them twisted his stomach.

"Rachel, it couldn't be helped. We knew this was going to be dangerous. So many people are already dead because of her that adding one more to the list can't be that surprising."

Rachel's long, red hair fell in waves around her face as she shook her head.

She looks so much like her mother. Down to the same guilt in her eyes. She doesn't deserve it, but it's there.

"But someone so well-known?" Rachel pressed. "It's exactly what we can't handle, right now. McNaire already wants my head on a spike."

"He'll have to go through me, first."

The corner of her mouth twitched up in a half-smile, and she replaced the cup on the table without drinking form it. The sounds of early-morning coffeehouse chatter filled the air, and for a moment, that was all Andrew heard. Rachel watched him closely for several seconds and then slipped her hands from his, instead folding them in her lap.

"Not here," she said.

Andrew frowned. "Rachel, I don't understand why you won't—"

"Because it's not safe. We're in enough danger as it is without the world finding out about this."

"Is it wrong that I don't care?"

Rachel closed her eyes. "Soon. I promise."

"I know you!"

The voice drew the pair's focus away from their hushed conversation. Beside their table stood a middle-aged woman with frizzy, greying hair. Her gaze was fixed on Rachel, whose expression was wary.

"Do you?"

The woman's head bobbed with her nod. "You're President Hartley's daughter! It's great to see you in New York. How's your mother?"

Rachel smiled thinly. "She's well, thank you."

Andrew's mouth twitched. He knew that was a lie.

Isabella was living at home under the constant supervision of a nurse after an attempt on her life shortly after the end of her second term in office. Some of her injuries had healed, but the attack had left her wheelchair-bound and traumatized. Andrew had accompanied Rachel on several occasions to visit her mother, and he knew she disliked discussing the matter.

"I hate to bother you, but could I have your autograph?"

Stiffly, Rachel nodded. "Sure. Do you have a pen?"

The woman began to dig through her purse. In her hurry, she dropped a pack of gum and a number of trinkets, which Andrew slid out of his chair and knelt to help her gather. She thanked him and set a pen and a napkin on the table. As Andrew retook his seat, Rachel signed the napkin and passed the pen back to the woman.

"Thank you very much. Take care."

"You too." Rachel stared off into the distance while the woman returned to her table.

She doesn't need to think about Isabella right now. It's only going to make her feel worse.

Andrew laid his hand on Rachel's. She blinked and glanced down at the point of contact before returning her attention to his face.

"I need to get to Washington and start on damage control," she said.

"Do you want me to come with you? I don't want you to have to deal with McNaire alone. Charlie said he's getting near the end of his rope with us."

Rachel shook her head. "No, I need you to stay here. Stay focused on your mission, Andrew. We'll get through this."

Rachel stood and pushed in her hovering chair before turning for the door. Andrew glanced at her coffee, which she had left untouched, and followed her to the exit. They stepped out onto the crowded Manhattan street, where hovercars passed by in congested, stacked layers of traffic.

"I'll keep you posted," said Andrew.

He kissed her swiftly on the cheek and turned away before she could comment, and they parted. Andrew started down the sidewalk, which was packed with people in the process of their morning commute. Andrew slipped through the crowd, his button-down shirt and slacks suggesting he was simply a member of the masses.

He followed the typical Manhattan bustle for a few blocks until his destination came into view. The angle of his approach had obscured exactly how large the cluster of people in front of Lawrence-Dodson Enterprises was, and as he took in the immensity of the crowd, he sighed.

And so it begins.

Andrew maneuvered between reporters from rival news stations and craned his neck for a better view of the platform that had been assembled for the press conference. He had arrived just in time; a tall man with a black business suit and hair nearly as dark had stepped onto the platform, flanked by security guards. The anxious buzz of the crowd died immediately as his presence was recognized, and a tense silence fell. The man's expression was troubled as he stepped behind the podium at the center of the platform.

Eddie Dodson. LDE co-president.

"As you are most likely aware..." Dodson said into the microphone adjoined to the podium, sparing a glance down at the place Andrew knew a screen would be projecting the speech. "Lawrence-Dodson Enterprises has suffered a tragic loss. Last night, July 25, 2232, my dear friend Damian Lawrence was murdered."

Dodson paused. Andrew pulled at the collar of his shirt, finding the tension surrounding him nearly as stifling as the summer heat.

"Damian's brother, Derek, returned this morning from a business trip to discover that Damian had been shot twice and that his wounds were fatal." Dodson closed his eyes, apparently collecting himself, and then opened them as he resumed speaking. "As of this moment, we do not have any leads as to who might be responsible, but I assure you that we are doing everything we can to find out. LDE's Manhattan facility will be closed to the public for the time being, pending further investigation of the crime scene. The production of androids will also cease until the police have had more time to get to the bottom of this."

A mass of hands shot into the air, but Dodson shook his head.

"I'm sorry, but that's all we know. No further comment will be given on the matter at this time. Thank you all."

The group of reporters exploded into shouts.

Why did she have to go after someone so well-known?

Andrew backed away into the crowd.

***

"The President will see you now."

"Thank you." Rachel inclined her head to the secretary who held open the door to the Oval Office.

Here goes nothing. She stepped inside, and the door whispered closed behind her.

Rachel knew this room far too well. For eight years, it had been her mother's office. This building had been her home. Now, it belonged to the man who had been the U.S. Secretary of Defense in her mother's cabinet.

The curtains were drawn save a sliver, where he stood, looking out the window onto the lawn. The sparse amount of light entering the room gave it a distinctly more eerie feeling than it had possessed in Rachel's childhood.

"I trust the 'situation' has been taken care of?"

Rachel bit her lip. "Not yet, Mr. President. We're working on it. We've been trying to find her for the last month, since her last trial at West Point."

"'Trying' and 'doing' are two different things, Rachel."

"I understand that, sir. We're doing the best we can."

"Well your *best—*" He slammed his palm against the wall just beside the window frame. Rachel flinched. "—isn't good enough."

He turned to face her, and she studied him apprehensively. Ethan McNaire had a commanding presence. He had silver hair that had once been dark, and cold, grey eyes that stared into Rachel's penetratingly.

"You disappoint me, Rachel. I gave you one task, *one*, to perform before your little 'Division' is disbanded permanently. And you couldn't even do that."

"I'm sorry." She tried to keep her voice even, devoid of emotion. Letting him see how much hearing the Division spoken of in such a way stung her would be a mistake.

McNaire had opposed the Division since its inception. '*Wars are meant to be fought by humans,*' he had said, '*not by machines.*' Though Rachel's mother had tried to explain that what the Division was doing was for the good of humanity, he had wanted no part in it. He'd been trying to disband the organization ever since, and now that he held the nation's highest office, he was on track to succeed.

After Mia was apprehended, the Division would be abolished for good. As the organization's current leader, Rachel was the one designated to incur McNaire's fury until their final mission succeeded.

"I'm not your mother, Rachel. I won't stand by and idly watch as that organization makes a mockery of everything this nation stands for. I won't allow such foolish practices to continue."

"With all due respect, *sir*," Rachel spat, "I'm not my mother, either. And I won't be pushed around by you. We will find the android, be assured of that. If you'll excuse me, I have business to attend to."

Without another word, she turned away and pushed open the door. As soon as she'd entered the lobby outside and the door had closed behind her, she heard her cousin's voice.

"How angry is he?"

"On what scale?"

Rachel knew Kat must've arrived just after she herself had. She doubted whatever McNaire had planned for the head of the Division's most decorated special operations team was any kinder, but he'd always seemed to hate Kat slightly less than he did her cousin.

Rachel surveyed Kat. Her hair was close-cropped but of a similar red, and she looked out of place in a pencil skirt and a tan blazer. Kat had joined the Army after college and entered as an officer, but she'd requested a transfer to Rachel's command upon realizing how dire the situation had become. Rachel trusted no one more to help her with the mission she'd been assigned.

"One to nuclear war," said Kat.

Rachel gave a small, tight smile. "I don't think he's quite ready to push the red button, yet. If he does, it will be a concentrated strike on me. I'll make sure he doesn't bring the rest of you down, too."

"Good luck with that one."

Rachel raised her eyes first to the secretary seated at her desk ignoring them and then to the three people standing several paces behind her cousin. She'd come to know the members of Kat's unit—Blue Team—well over the last few years. Casey O'Malley, a wiry, dark-skinned brunette with a sharp tongue and a wasp tattooed on the side of her neck, stood beside Charlie Vela, a young woman whose paleness was in stark contrast to her perpetually black wardrobe. Standing between the two was former Air Force pilot Lex Knight, who had spoken. He scratched at his burgeoning beard.

"I hope you don't honestly think we'd let you take the fall by yourself, Rachel," Lex continued. "That's not what we do."

Rachel gave a noncommittal shrug. She believed him, but she would deny that support, if given the choice. The Division was her burden to bear. Without her, the rest of these agents would still be living the lives they'd known before being recruited, and they would be much safer.

No, Rachel hadn't created the Division, but she felt as responsible for it as though she had.

"Thanks, Lex." She pulled in a deep breath and released it. "I explained to him that we have no proof she was actually involved in Damian Lawrence's death. We have our suspicions, and that's about it. She's still flying under the radar, and I don't think we'll find her until she wants to be found. That said, your mission still stands. If you find her, bring her back to base. If that isn't possible, destroy her."

"Understood." Kat nodded firmly.

***

Rachel stared at the holographic image projected above her desk with pursed lips, her arms folded over her chest.

"This is current?" she prodded, looking to Abigail Knight, her second-in-command.

"To the best of our knowledge, yes," said Abigail, raising a brow. She glanced from Rachel to the projection, taking a step closer to point to a spot on the miniaturized digital version of New York City. "We've managed to tap into the hardware we installed in them when they were created and use it to track them. That there? That's where Anubis was, the last time our intel was updated."

"When was that?"

"About an hour ago."

"Do you think they'll catch on?"

Abigail shrugged, her closely tailored suit-jacket rising and falling with her shoulders. "I wouldn't be surprised if they do. They've managed to evade us this long. If I had to guess, it's no accident that we've managed to find them right now. It isn't like we haven't tried to hack into their systems before—why would we suddenly succeed if something hadn't changed? Maybe they already know."

"And if they do and they want to be found," said Rachel, "that can't mean anything good for us."

"No, it can't." Abigail sighed heavily, her dark ponytail swinging behind her head as she shook it. "We've lost our target somewhere in New York. If the others are there, too, I really don't like what that could mean."

"If she's working with Osiris, then… I can't even begin to anticipate what kind of damage they could inflict." Rachel paused, her face falling as she realized how painful the repercussions would be for allowing something so horrible to come to pass. "Not a word of this to anyone connected with McNaire's office. Understood?"

Abigail nodded. "Of course." She turned and strode out the door, closing it behind her with a snap as she stepped into the hallway. As soon as she'd gone, Rachel sank into her chair, lowering her head into her hands.

See what you've done, Mom? I'm still cleaning up your mess.

Rachel recalled the day her mother had explained that the Division had tried again to create the perfect soldier after their first wave of androids had proven too deadly and unpredictable. She remembered how guilty her mother had looked when she'd explained that their second attempt–their last hope to save human lives by sending an android into combat instead–had failed so miserably that their new prototype had caused the deaths of a senator and his wife.

We never should have commissioned Mia. The others were enough of a problem. What do we do if they've found each other?

Rachel lifted her head to examine the projection once more. Six bright dots were spread throughout the city's display, each labeled with the name of the android linked to that location.

Osiris. Isis. Hathor. Horus. Bastet. Anubis.

"What the hell are you planning?" she muttered.

***

Andrew had not, despite the urging of Eddie Dodson, abandoned his–albeit undercover–post at LDE to leave the police to their investigation. On the contrary, he'd immersed himself in his work, hoping that doing so would distract him from his worries for Rachel and for the Division as a whole.

He'd been informed that Osiris and the other rogue androids had been located within New York City, and had he not already been perpetually armed, he would've begun carrying a weapon immediately. He glanced at his phone and the most recently updated projection of the androids' locations and then shut off the device, telling himself it didn't matter where they were.

If they wanted to find him, they would succeed, and his level of preparation would be irrelevant.

Movement caught his eye from one of the telesense screens to his left, and he froze.

It can't be. She wouldn't be that stupid.

Still, Andrew had to know. He leapt from his chair without a second's pause to run for the elevator, hoping with the entirety of his being that his target would still be in place by the time he arrived. As the elevator ascended, Andrew slipped a metallic disc no larger than the head of a pin from his pocket and pressed it tightly between his index finger and thumb, determined not to let it slip from his grasp until the proper time.

As the metallic doors slid open, he rushed from the elevator and into the corridor. He knew the offices of executives were located on this floor, and his target's presence here could not, he knew, be a good sign.

There. Almost too easy.

This thought seized him, stopping his foot from rising for the next step. His eyes flashed upward to find a woman with chin-length auburn hair striding toward him, her cold gaze fixed straight ahead as though he were thoroughly unworthy of her attention.

Was this too easy? She'd stepped into the open after

weeks of such a successful disappearance that many Division agents had started to lose hope that she would ever resurface, and of all places, she'd come *here*. Yes, Andrew reasoned, it was almost certainly a setup. But it was also the only opportunity he would probably have to slip the tracker onto her, and he would not waste the chance.

He started forward again, his steps deliberate and his focus on the empty air before him as he monitored her in his periphery. She gave no indication that she had noticed his presence, and it wasn't until his shoulder rammed hers that she cast her eyes in his direction.

"Sorry," he muttered, brushing off the jostled arm of his shirt and using the opportunity to drop the tracker into the bag she carried while her cold brown gaze was fixed on his face. She said nothing, turning away from him and continuing down the hallway, and Andrew started forward slowly, the knot in his chest beginning to unclench until a clear alto voice reached his ears from the elevator.

"You really should learn to be careful, Andrew."

He turned on his heel to face the elevator as the doors closed, sealing her within.

***

The wind brushed gently against Kat's face as she looked out on the city over the edge of the building upon which she was stationed. Her vantage point on the roof combined with the streetlamps and the neon signs adjoined to shops allowed her to see the entirety of the street below, which meant her part of the plan was working flawlessly.

She touched the earpiece situated just inside her right ear.

"This is Seward," she said. "Status report?"

"Knight. I'm in place on the roof across the street."

Kat's eyes flicked to the predetermined office building

opposite hers, and she spotted Lex slipping into position, half-concealed by its ledge. He saluted her before returning to the task of positioning his weapon.

"Agent Vela. Target in sight, prepared to pursue."

"O'Malley. Target has seen me. Ready to move on your mark."

Kat inhaled deeply and nodded to herself. "Okay. Go."

Her pulse raced as she withdrew her sidearm. She lacked the sniper rifle that Lex was using, but she always carried a weapon. In her line of work, it was imperative to be prepared. If everything went according to plan, Kat would have no need to fire.

But we're the Division. Nothing ever goes according to plan. It's better to be safe than sorry.

"This is Stark."

Kat frowned. Andrew was not a member of Blue Team, but he was a Division operative stationed in Manhattan. As such, he was linked to the communication network Kat's unit was using. He was not a part of their current plan, but he was aware of it. He'd been the one to slip the tracker onto their target.

"I'm signing off temporarily. I'm still at the office trying to dig up anything I can about her here, and I don't want to invite suspicion. I don't want to explain why the cameras would show me talking to myself."

"Understood," said Kat.

The line went dead. For several seconds, all was silent apart from the bustle of the street stories below where Kat stood.

Then Charlie's voice cut over the earpiece.

"Target is pursuing Agent O'Malley. I'm tailing them."

"Roger," said Kat. "Lex, do you have a shot?"

"Not yet."

"Keep watching."

"Of course."

Kat stepped onto the ledge at the building's extremity and grasped the nearest of the immense letters that formed the company's sign for support. One hand gripping the "O" in "Hover" and the other clinging to her gun, she looked down at the world below, searching out her colleagues in the dark and crowded street stacked with layers of traffic. She narrowed her eyes and scanned the ground to her right, in the direction of Casey and Charlie's last-known location.

"There."

Kat's eyes alit on Charlie in the crowd below her. She followed Charlie's gaze to woman walking purposefully several paces in front of her, and then Kat looked to Casey, who seemed to be performing well as bait. Casey gave no indication that she knew Mia was tailing her; she kept her focus forward and her hands away from the weapon Kat knew she'd concealed beneath her jacket.

"They're two blocks south. Lex, be ready," Kat ordered. "Casey's bringing them in fast."

"I told you your walk was unreasonably quick," muttered Charlie over the comlink.

"And you really think now's the time to point that out?"

"Ladies, enough." Kat sighed. "The task at hand, please."

"Sorry, Kat," they said in grudging succession.

"I see them," said Lex's excited voice in Kat's earpiece. "She's almost in range."

Kat's fingernails dug into her palms as she watched the group converge on her and Lex's location.

Maybe it'll work, she thought. *They're doing well so far.*

"Almost there... just a few more—damn it, Kat, she sees me!" hissed Lex.

Kat's chest constricted, and her heart began to pound in her ears. "What?"

"I don't know how, but she's looking right at me—"

"You're kidding, right?" demanded Charlie.

"That's not possible," Casey snapped.

"Casey, move! Get out of the—"

Lex's warning died in his throat. Mia, who had kept an equidistant pace between Casey and Charlie, had suddenly surged forward with preternatural speed and grabbed Casey by the back of the neck.

Kat's mind spun at a thousand miles per hour, scrambling for a solution. "Lex, take the shot."

"I don't *have* a shot! Casey's a human shield!"

"Charlie, get to them!"

"I'm trying, I–UMPH–" Charlie had shot toward the others the second Casey had been seized, but she wasn't quick enough. Mia reached back with her free arm and grabbed Charlie, tossing her headlong into the street.

"*No!*" cried Kat and Lex in unison.

The blaring of horns and shouts burst over the comlink, and Kat cringed and ripped it from her ear. She watched as Charlie utilized her extensive training to control the momentum of her fall and use it in her favor. She flipped to her feet, dodging and weaving through the vehicles until she reached Kat's side of the street.

Relief washed over Kat as she realized Charlie was safe. She replaced the comlink hastily in her ear.

"Lex!"

"Kat, she didn't even look at Charlie when she threw her! There is no shot!"

"Not for you."

Kat fired. A resounding *BANG* filled the air, echoing through the connected devices to assault Kat's ears in stereo. The shot fired from her gun hit Mia in the side, leading her to release Casey and clutch at the wound but not to fall.

"*Casey, get out of there!*" Kat shouted over the comlink.

Casey bolted forward at a dead run, turning at the nearby corner and disappearing into a crowd of people. Mia studied her newly acquired injury and the synthetic blood spilling from it, and by the time she looked up, Casey had vanished. Mia let out an enraged cry that echoed upward to where Kat stood.

"Abort," Kat demanded. "Everyone out, now."

"But Kat—"

"Charlie, not a word. Today is not the day."

Kat's eyes lingered on her target bitterly, on the deadly stare fixed on the spot where Casey had disappeared.

***

"You need to keep pressure on that," said Lex.

"It's not bleeding anymore. I'm fine."

Kat lingered several paces behind Charlie and Lex as the group moved through the halls of West Point, casting occasional sidelong glances at Casey, who hadn't said a word since the four agents had regrouped after the failure of their mission. Kat assumed Casey blamed herself for everything that had gone wrong, and Kat's attempts to assert otherwise had been unsuccessful. The group hadn't remained stationary long enough for Charlie to properly bandage the deep scrapes she'd received along her arm upon being thrown into the street, and the jacket she'd wadded into a makeshift bandage was soaked in scarlet.

"What happened?"

Kat clenched her jaw at the question and at the sound of high heels clicking angrily toward her from down the corridor. She looked ahead to find Rachel approaching. Kat pulled in a long breath and rolled her shoulders backward, and in moments, Rachel was at her side.

"She must've either known we were coming or just picked up on the plan way too quickly. She used Casey as a shield to block Lex's shot and almost got Charlie hit by a car."

"She knows who you are," said Rachel with a sigh. "All of you, I'd assume."

Kat's breath caught in her throat. "How is that possible?"

"I have no idea, but when Andrew planted the tracker on her, she addressed him by name. He wasn't at either of her trials, and they'd never spoken, so she must've gotten into our database."

"Didn't Andrew tag her at LDE?" asked Lex.

Rachel nodded. "He knew it was too easy. She's probably been playing us for quite a while. I just want to know what she's planning, but I'd settle for someone shooting her, already."

Kat sighed. "We'll catch her. Or kill her, whichever comes first. She's always been a problem, Rachel, and she always will be. The Division never should've commissioned her."

Rachel's lips pressed into a thin line, but she remained silent.

"Why don't we just have Andrew break cover and approach Dodson?" Kat pressed. "Odds are she never told him what happened during her last trial, and he could be in just as much danger as we are anytime we try to go after her. Look at what happened to Damian Lawrence. I doubt she'd think twice about turning on her creator."

"For now, the police investigation into Lawrence's death has bought us more time," said Rachel. "Go rest, all of you. Then we need a new plan."

***

"You know, I think you may be trying too hard, Andrew. I doubt they're paying you overtime."

Andrew's body tensed as thoroughly as it might have if he'd been suddenly turned to stone. His gaze slid slowly to the readout above his phone, which told him that all seven of the dots he should've been avoiding were far from the security room at LDE.

Apparently, technology could not be trusted.

"What do you want?" he asked, his hand moving reflexively for the gun at his belt. Before his fingers could close around the handle, a grip like iron enclosed his wrist and wrenched it backward until a sickening *snap* rang through the air. Andrew cried out as white-hot agony shot through his wrist, which was no longer within his power to bend. From his chair, he looked up into the sharp, cold face of Mia, the auburn-haired android his employers were responsible for unleashing and could not manage to destroy.

"I want you," she began, her tone low and deadly, "to tell Rachel something is coming that you will be powerless to stop. The Division thought it could control my kind and use us as servants. No more."

She dropped his wrist, which still throbbed in pain, and he let out a sharp breath, struggling to keep himself from reacting further.

"We are coming. You'll try to prepare, to anticipate us, but there's nothing you can do," she said, and her eyes flicked to his phone's display. All at once, the seven dots vanished. "Nothing but burn."

Andrew glanced upward once again, his eyes wide and his chest starting to constrict with panic, but she was gone.

FATED

At the sound of a knock on the front door, Desi tightened her grip on the mug of tea she held between her palms. She pulled her focus from the tea's brown ripples and exchanged glances with her brother Derek, who tensed. He slid off the sofa where he'd been sitting beside her and started for the door.

"Yes?" he called.

"It's Captain Scott Ryder, Mr. Lawrence. NYPD."

Her heart pounding at a sickening rate, Desi watched as Derek rolled his shoulders backward and opened the door. On the other side stood a uniformed man with greying brown hair whose mouth was pressed into a tight line.

"Sorry to bother you at home." The police captain cleared his throat and continued. "There, ah... there's a new development in your brother's case."

"Come in," said Derek. "Please."

He stepped back to allow Ryder to enter and then closed the door. Ryder inclined his head to Desi.

"Miss Lawrence," he said. "So sorry for your loss."

"Thank you," Desi muttered.

She had no idea how to begin to process the day's events. She'd awoken to thirty missed calls from friends and family members, and she'd turned on her telesense to find the robotics company her brothers ran with their friend plastered across every news channel along with the words, "DAMIAN LAWRENCE, SLAIN."

Desi had never been so numb, so sickened.

He's too young, she thought. *Was too young.*

Her mouth went dry, and she blinked away her thoughts to focus on the conversation at hand, which she realized had moved on without her. Derek settled onto the sofa at her side once more, and Ryder addressed him.

"Your company's security system recorded your brother's attack."

Desi squeezed the mug in an effort to still her trembling hands.

He can't let us see that, can he?

"Show me," said Derek. "Please."

Desi elbowed him hard in the ribs, and he let out a hiss.

"What the hell are you doing?" she whispered. "You really think you can handle that? That I can handle that?"

"You don't have to watch," he mumbled. "I'll tell you what I learn."

"I'm not going anywhere," said Desi. She watched him with her jaw set in determination until he turned back to the captain.

"Show us," Derek pressed.

Ryder produced his phone from his pocket and flicked it in the direction of the telesense set into the wall in front of where Desi and Derek sat. The main lobby of the Manhattan headquarters for Lawrence - Dodson Enterprises filled the screen.

The chandelier that brought life to the immense lobby during the day was dim, shrouding the foreground of the video in blackness. The back of the room was partially illuminated by a light from down the hall. As Desi watched, the light was interrupted by a shadow that grew rapidly larger as it moved toward the camera. When the figure came into view, only enough light touched the figure's outline to make it clearly that of a man. A dim red light flashed from somewhere in the video's foreground—Desi knew it meant the building was on lockdown. The security protocol had been activated, and no one would be able to get in or out until it was disabled.

The figure launched himself over the security desk. In the split second he was airborne, the light caught him at just the right angle to allow Desi to see his face. The man on the screen had light brown hair and eyes a few shades darker, and his face was lined with fear.

The face Desi had known her entire life but would never see again.

At the sound of Derek's gasp from beside her, Desi tore her gaze from their brother's face to scan the rest of the screen.

A woman approached the lobby from the corridor behind it. When she reached the room's edge, the fluid confidence of her motions gave way to an unsteady raising of her arms. The lobby's dim lighting made it difficult to tell, but Desi believed she recognized the smooth outline of a plasma gun in the woman's hands.

Caught by the glow of the streetlamps, Damian was clearer. While the woman's gun had been difficult to see, the one Damian had found was clearly visible in the light streaming through the row of glass doors at the lobby's front.

Damian launched himself at the doors and pulled on them to no avail. Desperately, he fired three times at the glass, but each time the plasma ricocheted uselessly and scorched a black mark in the polished marble floor. Damian turned back toward his pursuer, his hands raised in a gesture of pleading.

Another gunshot rang through the lobby.

The roar of Desi's pulse in her ears was nearly deafening, and she couldn't focus on what Derek and Captain Ryder were saying. She watched the woman on the screen take a few halting steps forward and fire again, and when the light of the streetlamps fell on the attacker's face, Desi felt her mug slip from her grasp and to the floor.

Lila.

She knew the sharp jawline and the pale blue eyes too well not to recognize the first android her brothers' company had created.

***

Desi stared at the woman standing before her. Ravenna's black clothing and hair nearly as dark made her stand out in Desi's unpainted entryway like a solitary inkblot on a blank page. Ravenna's face was more drawn than Desi remembered, her eyes lined with heavy circles as she studied Desi in turn.

She must be seeing him. I've always been told we look alike.

Desi knew calling her murdered brother's fiancée for this job had probably been a mistake, but she had no idea what else to do or where else she could turn.

"I'm so glad you're here," she said. "Please, come in."

She took Ravenna's arm carefully and led her into the apartment, closing the door behind them.

"I know I probably should've waited until morning, but I couldn't."

"It's not like you interrupted anything," said Ravenna.

Desi fiddled with the satin sash of her robe as she debated where to begin.

This was a terrible idea. All of it.

"Desi, nothing is going to make things right, again. I know you're going to try, and I appreciate it, but don't waste your breath."

Desi sighed. "I called you because, while I know you're right about that, I think I have something that comes as close to a solution as we could ask for. Before I explain, though, I want to ask you something." She slid onto a hovering stool at the breakfast bar and patted the seat beside her. When Ravenna had taken the seat, Desi continued. "When was the last time you accepted an offer involving someone's apprehension?"

Ravenna frowned and folded her arms across her chest. "Why are you asking me that?"

"I promise I'll explain. Just answer me, please."

Ravenna shook her head tightly. "I don't do that, anymore."

"What if I told you I knew who killed him?"

Several seconds of silence passed. Desi watched as Ravenna's fingernails dug into her folded arms, and with as pale as her knuckles were turning, Desi was surprised she hadn't drawn blood.

"I would sincerely hope you wouldn't joke with me about that."

"Rae, you know I'm not joking. I wouldn't have called you at this time of night if I didn't have a good reason, especially now. I wouldn't add to what you're already going through unless I thought it was completely necessary. Now, please, answer my question. If I told you I knew who was responsible, would you reconsider your 'retirement'?"

"Desi, if you had even the smallest hint pointing to someone with a millionth of a chance at guilt, I would chase them to the end of this Earth and make them suffer."

Desi blinked. After an instant's pause, she nodded. "That's how I hoped you would feel. Before I say anything about what I know, I need you to make me a promise."

Ravenna's eyes narrowed. "I never ask for much information about the promises I have to make," she said, "but that's vague even for me."

"Just promise that you won't kill her."

***

"Desi, are you okay? You look like you're a million miles away."

Desi blinked away the thoughts of Ravenna, Lila, and her brothers and did her best to return to the present time and place. She sat at a high table at the bistro she frequented with her friends, the concentrated gaze of whom bored into her, pressing her into her chair. Lucy sat to Desi's immediate left, the twist of her mouth concerned. Beside Lucy and across the table from Desi sat Marley, who chewed the edge of her lip as she watched Desi closely.

"I'm fine." Desi lifted her soda to her lips and sipped it while looking over the rim at the space between her friends. She had never been a good liar, as they'd often taken to telling her. She knew they would see through her feeble attempt. In the meantime, avoiding eye contact appeared to be the best course of action.

"You really don't need to lie," said Lucy. "We don't expect you to be yourself, right now. We just thought getting you out of your apartment might make you feel a little bit better."

Desi watched her glass thoughtfully as she lowered it to rest on the table. "I know, and I want you both to know that I appreciate it. I really do. It just... doesn't seem right to act like everything is still how it was."

"No one is asking you to," Marley said. "If you want to talk about anything, we'll listen."

Desi allowed herself a smile. "Thanks, Mar."

"It's what we're here for."

The touch of a gentle but unexpected hand on her shoulder caused Desi to jump. The others stared in alarm, but their expressions seemed directed more at her reaction than at the presence that had caused it.

"Hello, Desdemona."

She recognized that voice. It was a cool tenor with an air of dignity and poise, confidence and polite reservation. A fluttery feeling surged up through her stomach, and the skin of her shoulder tingled beneath the touch.

Why does it have to be him?

"Edward," she said coolly.

Desi kept her eyes facing pointedly forward, staring at the table just in front of where Lucy's hands were clasped. In her periphery, she saw her friends exchange glances. They began to shift, and her jaw clenched. She knew what was about to happen.

"I need to get back to my parents' hotel in time to meet them after their negotiations," said Lucy. "That shareholder keeps trying to buy them out."

"We took my car," added Marley. "I need to take Lucy back and meet my sister."

Desi closed her eyes and sighed. "You don't have a sister."

"Sister-in-law," Marley amended hastily. She and Lucy stood in messy succession and gave Desi quick goodbyes and a few more apologies for rushing off so hastily.

Desi said nothing. After her friends had scurried off, she let out a small breath and plastered on a smile.

"Would you like to take a seat?" she asked without looking at him.

"Thank you."

Into the seat Marley had just occupied slid a man wearing a business suit. Desi realized that for the sake of decorum she needed to stop deliberately avoiding his gaze, and she lifted hers away from the table. He was watching her with kindness in his grey eyes.

Desi had never been able to fully understand the way she felt about Edward Dodson. She resented him for being closer to her brothers than she was, though she knew that was petty and she had trouble admitting it even to herself. He had never been anything but the image of politeness and propriety to her—at least until a night several weeks earlier—which led her to wonder sometimes if he had any flaws at all. His was the presence that had always been near but just distant enough to be inaccessible, and therefore as irritating as it was intriguing.

And then she'd slept with him.

"Was there something you wanted to talk about?" she asked. She forced her expression to remain even and calm, betraying nothing of her thoughts.

He was watching her carefully, searching her. It was as though he saw through her, past the façade she had so meticulously devised. Perhaps he knew her as well as she believed she knew him, and neither of them would admit to trying to solve the riddle of the other.

"I wanted to see if you were all right." The words and the sympathy in his eyes were genuine.

"I'm wonderful." Desi was grateful for the make-up hiding the puffiness around her eyes. She'd found it difficult to sleep, but he didn't need to know that.

"Forgive me for saying so, but your face says otherwise." She frowned and prepared to fire a pointed reply, but he hurried on before she had the chance. "It looks as lovely as always, but you can't hide sadness with eyeshadow."

Desi felt her cheeks begin to burn.

"There's nothing wrong with allowing yourself to hurt. I hope you know that."

She opened her mouth to speak, but no answer would come. Instead, she replied with a small shrug.

"I wanted to tell you," Eddie went on, "that if you decide you need to talk with someone about any of this, or about anything else, then I would be more than happy to listen."

"I... don't know if that's wise."

A hand passed in front of Desi, lowering onto the table the pasta she'd ordered when her friends had been present. The confused waitress paused with the other plates balanced precariously on her arms, glanced at Eddie, and then gave Desi a confused look.

"My friends had to deal with an emergency," she explained with unconcealed bitterness. The waitress glared and nodded. She then plastered on a smile and looked to Eddie expectantly.

He shook his head. "Nothing for me, thank you."

The waitress's smile vanished, and she departed in a huff with the surplus food. A moment of silence passed, and then Desi resumed her careful study of Eddie's face. He seemed to be trying for calm, but the set of his jaw told her he was bracing for a hurricane. She let out a long breath.

"What do you want from me?" she asked quietly.

She felt a warm touch on the hand that rested beside her untouched silverware. She watched as Eddie moved to the seat beside her.

"For you to stop pushing me away," he said softly. "Desdemona, I don't know why you're so determined to pretend there's nothing between us. I want you to let me be there for you. Talk to me. I know you have to be suffering, and that kills me."

"Why?"

She kept his eyes on his and did not pull back when she felt his hand against her cheek.

"Do you honestly not know how I feel about you?" he asked.

Desi opened her mouth to reply, but no words would come. Before she could find the ability to push them from her lungs, he leaned forward and kissed her.

Her heart seemed to stop beating.

Desi felt the warmth of sunlight on her face and of arms enclosing her waist. She felt the rise and fall of a chest pressed to her back and the soft touch of satin sheets against her bare skin.

She blinked away the temptation of returning to sleep in this enveloping comfort. As she turned her head to take in her surroundings, her heart leapt into her throat.

I couldn't have.

Eddie slept beside her, his dark hair tousled, his face peaceful and handsome and content. The ghost of a smile graced his lips, and Desi fought down the urge to lean closer and wake him with a kiss.

How could she have done this? Eddie was her brothers' best friend—how could she have risked damaging their relationship? Her stomach turned. Would Damian and Derek still trust Eddie, if they knew? Would they still trust Desi?

You're overreacting, she told herself. *They want you both to be happy. If this is what you want, they have to support you. But is it what you want?*

She watched Eddie sleep for a moment longer and then slid out from under his arm. The hardwood floor was cold beneath her feet, and she moved quickly to retrieve her clothes, desperate to be anywhere else.

She pulled back, uncertain and more than a little afraid. She wanted to be alone to process the tornado everything had been since Damian's death, but she wanted to be with Eddie.

I can't make these kinds of decisions right now.

"I'm sorry, I have to go." She slipped her hand out of his and stood. He watched her with a composite of alarm and regret.

"I—I'm sorry, Desi. I—"

"Desdemona."

"Desdemona." He closed his eyes. "I don't know—"

"Please don't apologize. I'm sure you, ah—don't you have an investigation to keep track of? Derek isn't in the mental state to be… messing with any of it."

"Yes, you're right." He opened his eyes and looked into hers, and her stomach twisted with guilt.

"Goodbye, Edward."

Desi turned away, unwilling to see more of the hurt she had caused him. Under her breath as she strode from the table, she muttered, "What have I done?"

***

Desi sat at the end of her sofa, her head in her hands. She couldn't stop mentally replaying the call she'd received from Ravenna.

"I lost her."

Pulling in a deep breath, Desi considered her next words carefully. She still wasn't thoroughly convinced by what Derek had told her, but she had to trust him enough to give his plan a chance.

"Rae," she began at last, "there was someone else in the room when my brother was killed. Derek thinks it... well, it might not have been all Lila's fault."

"Even if there was someone else there, how does that adjust the blame? Lila pulled the trigger, Desi!"

"I don't know exactly what Derek thinks this is going to change, but I don't think we can assume anything without understanding every fact at our disposal. We both know things aren't always as they—"

"I have to go. I'll call you soon."

"Rae, wait, I—"

The conversation had ended so abruptly that Desi's already paramount confusion and despair had escalated into all-consuming helplessness. There was nothing left for her to do. Everything rested on Derek, now. If Ravenna wouldn't listen to her... Desi could only pray she would listen to him.

Nausea rolled through Desi's stomach. Derek was all she had left. She couldn't allow anything to happen to him. If Lila had somehow been coerced into killing Damian as Derek suspected, she was still dangerous, as was whoever was responsible for forcing her hand. If Derek was wrong, Lila could just as easily kill him next.

And what can I do? He's decided he's going after her, and there's nothing I can say to convince him to stop.

Desi sat still, forcing deep breaths and trying to slow her pulse. She closed her eyes against the tears prickling at her eyes, but they refused to be held at bay. She wiped them away and reached for the phone resting on the end table.

This is a bad decision. Very bad.

She reached for the phone resting on the end table.

***

"What's going on, Desi?" asked Eddie. He took a sip from the coffee mug she'd given him, and she left her own untouched on the table.

"I just don't know what do to, anymore. Ravenna won't listen to me, and Derek is convinced that Lila isn't guilty. He's been studying the security footage. He says someone else was there when Damian was killed and that Lila was moving so jerkily that it was like she wasn't under her own control. I hired Ravenna to bring Lila back in one piece, but I know she wants to kill her. If Derek is right and it isn't Lila's fault, what if I'm responsible for her death? I don't want anyone else to die, Eddie!"

He pulled in a long breath and set his mug on the table in front of the sofa as he reached for her hand and traced its back with his thumb.

Desi couldn't stop herself from shivering under his touch.

"Come here," Eddie said gently. He pulled her closer and slid an arm around her.

Desi kept her posture rigid for a moment, and then she relaxed with a sigh, resting her head against his chest as she embraced him.

"Thank you for being here," she said quietly. "I really don't think you understand how much it means to me."

"I meant it when I said I'd always be here." Eddie traced her back gently with his fingertips, and her grip on his shoulders tightened.

"Why?" asked Desi. "Why me? You honestly think I deserve someone like you?"

"Someone like me?" he repeated, frowning.

"You know what you're doing with your life, Eddie. You always have. You're brilliant, and the world loves what you've done at LDE. You could have someone who does something substantial instead of going to one audition a month because she can't stand getting rejected and didn't get arrested for being shitty at handling her liquor."

Eddie laughed softly and rested his hand against her cheek, guiding her gaze upward. When their eyes met, he gave her a small smile.

"It's always been you," he said. "Since you got back from school and just seemed to glow with how much you love to act even though it breaks your heart. You're made of passion and love, even if you don't see it. You feel things in a way I've never seen in anyone else. You care with your whole heart. Even when you try to pretend you don't."

She watched him, taking in the affection in his eyes. She opened her mouth to speak but realized she had no idea what to say. Instead, she let out a quick sigh, pulled him closer, and kissed him.

Eddie's hand slid downward to rest at the small of her back as his lips caressed hers. Desi's heart pounded as her fingertips brushed against his chest through the thin material of his shirt, and he traced her jaw and slid his fingers into her hair.

She slid closer, and Eddie guided her onto his lap as their kisses grew more fervent with each passing moment.

When Desi eventually pulled back and rested her forehead against his, she felt the rapidness of his breath against his lips. They tingled at the touch.

"I…" Desi swallowed. "We both need rest."

Eddie nodded. "You're right," he said with a nod. "I'll head home before it gets later."

"No," she said quickly. She gave his shoulder a squeeze. "I don't want you driving this late when… when it's not safe."

Eddie slipped his hand from where his fingers had tangled themselves in her hair and interlocked his fingers with hers.

"What would you like me to do?" he asked.

"You can stay here. I'll… go get pillows."

Desi squeezed his hand and released it as she slid off of him and to her feet. She hurried into her bedroom to retrieve a pair of pillows and a heavy blanket, and when she returned, she passed them to Eddie. He thanked her and laid the pillows at one end of the sofa before draping the blanket over himself as he lay back.

"Please help yourself to anything you want," said Desi, gesturing toward the kitchen. "I'll be… in there, if you need me."

"Thank you," Eddie said again.

"Goodnight," said Desi. "Lights."

At her word, they turned off, and Desi departed for her bedroom without another word.

***

I shouldn't be here.

Damian's visitation service had been held in the company's headquarters, as requested in his will. Derek and Eddie had left as soon as the service had concluded. Desi knew Derek was off somewhere trying to find evidence of Lila's innocence, and she hadn't bothered telling him how clear it was that he was in over his head.

Instead, Desi had focused all her efforts on slinking off into the building when everyone had gone their separate ways. She'd made her way upstairs to Damian's old office and to his computer.

Now, she tapped the projected display before her, sifting through the company's multitude of files and programs and making her way to the security footage.

Thank God I needed to order a plane ticket the last time I was here. If I didn't have his password…

She drew in a long breath.

I have to know. I need to see what Derek saw, and not the shortened version the cops showed us. Ryder doesn't want us to worry; he wouldn't want us to know, if there was someone else in the clip that they had no leads on. If Derek says that file exists, I will find it.

After a few tedious minutes of scraping through files, Desi succeeded in locating the video. Then, steeling herself to what she was about to see, she touched the words *"7-25-2232, 11:15 PM."*

A red box popped up on the display, *"The most recent version of the file, '7-25-2232, 11:15 PM' is unavailable."*

Desi frowned. "I don't know why I expected any differently," she muttered.

Another message followed.

"File information suggests that the most recent version was edited. Attempt to locate original?"

Desi raised an eyebrow and tapped "Yes."

"File located."

Desi swallowed and played the clip.

On the screen, the lobby was dark and barren. The only light came from down the hall, toward the lab where androids were designed and modified, and it was muted.

A shadow passed in front of the light.

This is it.

The shadow grew larger and was caught by the streetlamps, and Desi's stomach lurched at the sight of the fear in her brother's eyes.

Damian dove behind the security desk, surfacing again with a plasma gun in hand. Desi glanced between her brother and Lila, who had just appeared at the back of the room. She, too, had a gun.

Damian shot at the glass doors, but the plasma bolts only ricocheted backward, nearly crashing back into Damian each time he fired.

"Plasma-resistant," breathed Desi.

"*No!*" screamed someone on the video. One glance toward the source of the voice told Desi that it had been Lila. Damian lay on the ground now, his back against the door. His leg was bleeding profusely just above the knee.

"You don't have to do this, Lila," said Damian.

Desi was only vaguely aware of the tears streaming

down her face as she watched her brother plead for his life.

"You don't have to–" Damian's gaze drifted over Lila's shoulder, toward someone or something in the background. "Just remember who you are. Remember who I–"

Lila fired again.

Damian lay motionless, slumped against the door.

"No. No, no, no." But Desi knew that no matter how many times she said it–how many times she denied it, wished with every fiber of her being that it wasn't true–the word would not bring her brother back.

"You've done well," said a voice on the video.

That sounds like... No, it doesn't.

Desi denied the train of thought that had begun and focused on the screen as her pulse pounded.

"What have I done?" asked Lila. She spun around, aiming the gun at the previous speaker, whom the shadows concealed. "What have you done to me? *Help him!*" she screamed.

"You've done your part," said the man still hidden in shadow. "Deactivate."

Lila fell to the ground instantly.

He was right, Desi thought over and over as her breathing slipped from her control and panic dripped ice cold through her veins. *Derek was right. It wasn't her fault.*

There was silence in the lobby. After a moment, the man stepped forward to pick up Lila from the floor where she had fallen.

Desi's breath caught in her throat as the sparse light from the street outside fell across Eddie's face.

SHATTERED

Lila wove through the crowded streets at a pace barely under a run. She didn't want to draw attention to herself by moving as fast as she needed to, but it grew increasingly more difficult to hold herself back.

It would only be so long before Derek began to tear the city apart searching for her. She was already almost certain she'd murdered his brother, Damian.

There are too many people looking for me, Lila thought. *I'll never be safe.*

She felt the plasma bolt before she saw it.

There was a disruption in the air to her left, and then she felt something hurtling toward her. She acted on pure reflex, leaping out of the way and whipping around to face her attacker. Her gaze flitted to the fourth floor of a structure on the opposite side of the street: a large, extravagant hotel. The shooter didn't linger, but Lila was absolutely certain she saw a flash of dark hair disappear from the window.

She had to go. Immediately.

Lila instantly resumed her path, this time moving at what seemed to be her natural speed. There was no time to waste playing human, not when one of her many pursuers had at last made an attempt on her life.

Life? Is that what this is?

Her feet carried her to the skyscraper ahead of their own accord.

As she stood in its shadow, she took in a deep breath, struggling to understand why she had come here. She studied the building, allowing its beauty to envelop her even as she understood that it was the last place on Earth she needed to be. The walls were made of glass, and there were eighteen stories stretching toward the sky.

Lila cast a long glance over her shoulder and then returned her focus to the head office of Lawrence-Dodson Enterprises. Somehow, her subconscious had guided her here when it had realized the danger of her situation.

"They made me," she muttered. "Maybe something here can fix me."

She peered in through the glass front doors. The lobby was deserted.

Good. She breathed a sigh of relief. *If someone was here, they would've called the police on me by now.*

She examined the building's exterior from her vantage point at its foot, her desperation escalating by the second as she realized that this wasn't going to be easy. Another glance inside at the lobby and she saw a camera watching her. She gave a halfhearted tug at the handle of the door on her right and wasn't surprised when it remained stationary. The front doors wouldn't be an option unless she wanted to risk setting off whatever security system the building had.

Without consciously deciding to run, she found her feet moving again. Perhaps a part of her knew what she was doing after all. As she dashed around the building, she was astonished by her own superhuman speed and surveyed the walls for another entrance.

The building's rear came into view along with a door. A quick tug on the handle when she reached it told her that this one was locked, too, but she squeezed the handle tightly and then wrenched it with all her might. To her surprise, it twisted, the door swinging open with a groan.

If they're already looking for me, I can't imagine breaking in is going to worsen whatever sentence awaits. And if the security system tells someone I'm here, it's not like I can't outrun them.

The lights turned on automatically upon her entrance, illuminating a thin hallway that widened into a circular space with doors leading in every direction. Lila sighed. She followed the hall and stepped tentatively into the circular room, looking around for some clue that might lead her to what she needed to know.

A cylindrical device sat at the room's center. Raising an eyebrow, Lila took a step toward it. In under a second, the device came to life. Lila jumped. A microprojector in the object's center flicked on, emitting a three-dimensional map of the building. It was tinted blue, and it displayed each of the building's eighteen floors in great detail.

"Welcome to Lawrence-Dodson Enterprises," said a smooth, automated female voice presumably emitted by the map. "What are you looking for today?"

Lila blinked. *Can it really be that easy?*

"The office of Derek Lawrence." She winced, hoping that the device didn't have voice-recognition programming.

"Right this way," said the computer, and Lila breathed a sigh of relief. The projection of the building changed; a path to the top floor now glowed, illuminated in a bright white light. She studied the image for a few moments and then turned to the door that she now knew would lead her to Derek's office. Her efforts at memorization proved pointless, however, when panels along the walls in the new hall she followed began to glow.

This is too good to be true. Where's the catch?

Lila wove through the building, following the path the computer laid out for her. She finally decided that perhaps nothing would go wrong—that her good fortune in finding Derek's office without any obstacles in her path was karmic repayment for the loss of the memories she was slowly regaining.

I guess even murderers have good days.

In front of Derek's office door, she stopped.

No. No matter how many times you call yourself that, she thought, *it's not going to change anything. Even if you're guilty, it's... not worth it to put yourself through more than the rest of the world already is.*

She thought of Derek's friend and business partner Eddie, who had announced her guilt to the world at a press conference. She thought of Ravenna, Damian's fiancée, who had lost the man she loved and who had been hunting Lila ever since she'd heard of her potential guilt.

Stop, Lila told herself. *Breathe.*

She opened the door and stepped into the room. She stood opposite a glass wall, which was all that separated this room from the outside world. To her right, two filing cabinets stood in the corner between the glass wall and one made of a more substantial material, presumably steel, on which a telesense was mounted. To her left, against another wall, was a desk, cluttered as it was with various papers and file folders and pictures of what had to be Derek's family.

She advanced on the desk, gingerly lifting a photoscroll that lay face-down. Immediately, she regretted this decision. The first photo that appeared on the screen was of three people. Derek stood on the left, with a woman to the immediate right that had to be his sister Desdemona, as they shared the same blue eyes, small noses, and high cheekbones. On the photo's far right stood a man that Lila instantly knew, though the reason for this recognition was unclear. She trailed her fingertips over the image, racking her brain for anything that might help her remember.

Then it hit her with force.

Lila stood in a room she had looked into only ten minutes previously: the lobby of Lawrence-Dodson Enterprises. It was dark—the only light came from behind her. She felt something cold and smooth in her hand, and she glanced down to see that she was holding a gun.

In front of her, he was slumped against the door.

Damian.

There was no sound in the room. Damian's lips moved, but she couldn't hear what he was saying. Lila felt the muscles of her hand tighten involuntarily, and she squeezed the trigger.

The photoscroll fell from her hands and onto the floor, where the screen shattered.

She turned her attention to another object on the desk: Derek's computer. As she perched on the edge of the chair in front of the desk, the computer turned on automatically.

Lila frowned, examining the desktop wallpaper. It was a photo of five people. Desdemona stood on the far left, with Derek beside her. On the far right was Eddie, wearing a business suit, with Damian to his left. And in the center was... Lila.

"They all trusted me," she breathed. "What have I–?" She cut herself off with a shake of her head. *Don't do this to yourself.*

"Why would you come back here?"

Lila's mechanical heart leapt into her throat.

Slowly, she pushed herself to her feet and turned toward the voice. In the doorway stood a woman in a grey blazer with chin-length auburn hair. She watched Lila with a raised brow, leaning against one side of the doorframe as her palm rested against the other, effectively blocking Lila's path.

"I was just on my way out," said Lila as she took a tentative step toward the woman and the exit.

"You're determined to be caught, aren't you?"

"What are you talking about?" Lila took another step toward the door as her fingers curled on reflex toward her palms, her nails biting into her skin. "Who are you?"

"I'm you," she said. "But better."

In a blur, the woman shot forward. Suddenly, she was in front of Lila, and then her hand was closing around Lila's throat and lifting her from the floor. Lila struggled for breath. She scrambled for a decent grip on the woman's fingers and worked to pry them away from her neck, but the woman wouldn't budge.

"You're going to bring this down on all of us. I knew we should've gotten rid of you."

She tossed Lila away from her as easily as she might toss a ragdoll.

The moment her back impacted with the glass wall, Lila cried out in agony. Shards embed into her skin as she broke through it and began to fall. In a desperate attempt to right herself, Lila used her preternatural speed to flip herself over. She clung to the floor of the office as her body swung forward and slammed into the glass of the floor beneath the room in which she'd just been standing.

As she heard the blare of horns below her, she chanced a glance downward to see the four vertical layers of traffic racing past LDE. Fourteen stories separated her from the highest level of traffic.

Get up. Get up and get past her.

Lila's pulse pounded at a sickening pace in her ears. Above her head, she heard the crunch of glass beneath her attacker's feet and processed for the first time that the majority of Derek's office wall had been obliterated. She tore her focus from the cars below. The instant the woman appeared above, bending over the ledge with a scowl, Lila hoisted herself upward. Her muscles screamed as she propelled herself back into the office and slammed headlong into her attacker.

The two women tumbled to the floor. Lila felt her attacker's hand at her throat again and grabbed a shard of glass from the carpet, wincing as it sliced into her hand. She stabbed the woman's arm, and when she heard a hiss and felt the woman's hand release her, Lila pushed herself to her feet and ran for the door.

If the alarms didn't go off when I entered, someone's bound to know I'm here, now. I need to get out.

Lila hurtled into the hallway but was stopped when she felt the woman's grip on her shoulder. Without hesitation, she whipped around and drove her fist into the woman's stomach.

The woman laughed.

Lila frowned and swiped her leg in an attempt to take out the woman's, but the move failed. She struck another blow into her attacker's abdomen next, but as she pulled her wrist backward, her attacker caught it.

"You're holding back," said the woman. "Why the hell would you do that?"

She slammed her fist into Lila's ribs so hard Lila flew three doorways down the hall before she crashed to the floor.

Lila's back ached where her spine had impacted the tile, and her shirt clung to her by virtue of the warm blood she could feel sticking to her skin.

"Why do you care?" she demanded as she struggled to stand. "What am I to you?"

"An inconvenience."

The woman charged at her, and this time, Lila had had enough. She launched herself at her attacker and delivered a punch to her chest that knocked the breath from the woman's lungs and sent her flying past Derek's office. Lila watched as the woman's head hit the floor. She let out a groan but said nothing, and then she was still.

Lila's stomach twisting with guilt, she briefly debated going to help the woman. She hated the thought of hurting people.

But she has to be an android, too. That's the only way she could hurt me so badly. She'll be fine.

Reminding herself that she herself had launched from her hotel room and landed on the roof of a car with scarcely a scratch to show for it, Lila turned away from the woman and made her way to the elevator. As soon as the doors closed behind her, she leaned against the wall and mentally surveyed her injuries. She knew she was losing blood—or whatever her creators had given her to pass for it—rapidly, but she had no idea where to turn.

I'm going to be fine. I'm going to be fine.

She reached back to determine how deep her cuts were, and when she realized her fingers were drenched in red, she processed exactly how dizzy she had become. The elevator dinged and halted, and Lila's knees buckled. She fell to the floor just as the doors opened.

As the edges of her vision grew dark, she saw Derek running toward her across the lobby. She then saw only black.

***

As he rushed through the hallway toward his apartment, Derek kept Lila as close to his chest as he could. She was still unconscious, his sunglasses concealing her face to the extent that they could. He knew allowing her to be seen in public would be a disaster neither of them could afford.

The warmth of her blood covering his hands set his body buzzing with fear.

He fumbled with the doorknob of his apartment, the slickness of blood making it difficult to get a solid grip. Mentally cursing whoever had done this to Lila, he at last managed to push open the door and enter his apartment. He stumbled over the threshold and shouldered the door closed behind him.

"You're going to be okay," he mumbled.

He carried Lila through the living room and past the portraits of his family—Damian seemed to be judging him from the frame beside the telesense—on the way to his bedroom. When he arrived, he laid her down carefully on the left side of the bed and took stock of her injuries. Her throat was lined with finger-shaped red marks, and Derek circled the bed to examine the wounds on Lila's back. His stomach lurched at the sight. There were deep gashes tracing her shoulder blades and spine, and her shirt had been all but shredded on this side.

"Who did this to you?"

The first thought to pass through his mind was the simplest answer: Ravenna. But he knew she wouldn't have allowed Lila to walk away, if she'd found her.

Derek sighed and made his way into the bathroom. He opened the cabinet below the sink and retrieved a stack of towels, and then he returned to the bedroom to pull a small metal cylinder from his bedside table.

Sitting at the edge of the bed behind Lila, Derek gingerly raised the torn fragments of her shirt and wiped away the blood covering her skin as gently as he could. When the first of his white towels had been saturated with blood, he let it fall to the floor and used the second to dab gently along the cuts. He set the towel aside and lifted the laser he'd retrieved from the drawer.

"I'm sorry," he whispered.

He pressed the black button on the cylinder's side, and a red beam erupted from it and into the cut lining Lila's right shoulder blade. Her body twitched, and Derek winced.

"I'm sorry," he repeated.

He guided the beam along the cut, and he watched as the wound sealed. If Lila were awake, Derek knew she would object to this form of repair; he'd only ever used it while she was unconscious, and it had only been necessary a handful of times since her activation.

Derek couldn't stand the idea of using his position as one of Lila's creators against her. He'd always refused to— he'd never so much as installed an upgrade without her permission. He hated using a laser to mend her without the opportunity to ask her if it was what she wanted.

I don't have a choice. I can't take her to one of our labs. It's not safe for her out there.

He muttered apologies he knew she couldn't hear as he cauterized each of her wounds and then gently wiped off the remaining blood with a wet cloth. When he'd finished and disposed of the towels, he washed his hands and returned to the bed, where he sat down beside Lila.

He inhaled deeply and gave her hand a soft squeeze.

***

Why do I feel like I've been run over?

Lila stirred, moving her limbs one at a time to gauge what state her body was in and finding that while she was sore essentially everywhere, nothing hurt more than her back. She reached for her shoulder blade through the shredded back of her shirt and winced when the contact stung.

Does that feel… somewhat healed?

She trailed her fingertips over the area and bit her inner cheek against the pain. Just as she'd suspected, the wound no longer felt open; her skin had sealed.

Despite the pain coursing throughout her body, she processed that she was lying on something soft and comfortable. She opened her eyes to find herself in an unfamiliar bedroom. The plush comforter beneath her was blue and pulled up high enough to conceal the sheets from her view, and the nightstand and armoire were wooden and dark brown.

Lila lifted her head from the pillow slowly and sat up, holding back a hiss as her body protested. Her gaze fell on a folded tan sweater lying beside her, and she pulled it on over her shirt.

Straightening the three-quarter sleeves of her sweater, she stood and made her way for the door opposite the bed. When she opened it, she found herself facing a living room she recognized.

Derek found me?

In a rush, Lila's mind was flooded with images of the other android and being thrown through a glass wall, nearly falling from LDE's top floor. She remembered seeing Derek's face before collapsing in the elevator.

He saved me.

"You're awake!"

At the sound of a loud clang, Lila shifted her focus to the kitchen, where Derek had evidently just dropped a plate. He sighed and retrieved it from the floor, setting it on the counter before hurrying across the apartment to Lila's side.

"How are you feeling?" he asked. His sandy hair was tousled and the circles beneath his eyes were dark.

"Better. What happened?"

"You—here, come sit down."

He guided her to the sofa, and when she sat at one end, he took the other.

"Did you seal the cuts?" Lila asked, folding her hands in her lap.

Derek nodded. "I'm sorry, I–I wanted to discuss it with you before I did anything, but I had no idea how long it would take for you to wake up, and you were losing so much blood. I didn't know if waiting any longer would be safe."

As he spoke, Lila watched his eyes. She was captivated by the warmth in their blue depths even when he was sitting so far from her; it seemed as though he wanted to reach for her, but he only leaned slightly forward where he sat.

"It's okay," said Lila. "Thank you. You didn't have to do that, you didn't…"

She recalled how desperate he'd been to stop her from leaving and how frightened he'd looked as he'd hurtled toward her in the elevator.

"I… really don't think you could've done this," he'd told her before she'd left. *"Not to Damian."*

Lila's eyes stung with tears. She lowered her head into

her hand.

"What's wrong?"

At the sound of his concern, she could hold herself back no longer. She lifted her head and wrapped her arms around him tightly.

"Thank you," she muttered. "Thank you."

He was still for a moment, and then he rested his hand against her back.

***

Derek sat hunched over his desk. He'd ignored the police tape restricting entry to his office; he didn't care that the glass wall had been replaced by poorly assembled temporary panels held together by thick silver tape. His brother's visitation service was slated to begin shortly, and it would be held on the company's first floor, just as Damian had wanted.

Would he have written his will differently if he'd known he'd die here?

Derek pulled in a long breath through his nose and released it through his mouth.

He remembered the first breath Lila had taken. He remembered the pride in Damian's eyes when the android they'd designed with their best friend had opened her eyes. He remembered when she'd walked through the front door of his apartment with a birthday cake and he'd realized for the first time how beautiful she was—the way her golden hair caught the light, how her smile was the most infectious one he'd ever seen.

I shouldn't feel this. I shouldn't feel anything for her.

Not only did he have footage of Lila shooting his brother through the chest, but he'd created her. He couldn't allow himself to give in to the urge to let himself love her.

Could he?

He'd seen a shadow at the back of the security video.

He knew someone else had been present the night of his brother's murder. He knew how choppy and forced Lila's movements had been even as she'd raised the gun, like she'd been fighting herself.

Derek couldn't force himself to believe that she was truly responsible. There had to be another explanation.

"Derek?"

He looked up to find his business partner standing just outside his office door, beyond the line of tape Derek had slipped past to reach his desk. Eddie's dark hair was combed back neatly, and his suit was pressed so crisply that he might've been preparing for a wedding and not a funeral.

"Are you–? I know you aren't all right," said Eddie, "but is there anything I can do?"

Derek shook his head and pushed his chair backward as he stood.

"Let's just get this over with," he said.

***

As the handle of the gun made contact with the junction of her neck and the back of her head, Lila reached out to catch herself on Derek's coffee table. Pain splintered through her skull and white spots flashed through her vision.

She looked up into the pointed, enraged face of Damian's fiancée.

"I knew he had to be hiding you here," Ravenna growled.

Lila forced herself to her feet and moved as rapidly as her enhanced speed would allow to stand behind Ravenna and twist her arm until she released the gun with a sharp cry.

"I never wanted to hurt anyone," said Lila. "I need you to understand that."

"You *killed* him!"

Ravenna whipped her leg backward and knocked Lila's out from under her. As her head swam and her balance faltered, Lila crashed to the floor.

She knew she could easily best Ravenna, if she allowed herself to try. But she had no intention of harming anyone else, least of all someone whose life she'd ruined.

She deserves to avenge him. And I deserve whatever she does to me.

As the pain pulsing through Lila's head intensified, the room around her blurred.

Lila attempted to lift her hand, but her arm refused even to twitch at her command. Her body was leaden, pressing her down to the cold, metal surface she felt beneath her bare arms.

"And if it doesn't work? If she remembers, afterward?"

"She won't. You should be more confident, by now. Her programming will require her to obey, and then her mind will be wiped."

Lila struggled to open her mouth to address the voices coming from either side of her—the first was male, the second female—but neither her jaw nor her tongue would move.

She heard the air shift from her left side, in the direction of the male voice, and then a sharp sigh and the clattering of metal against another surface.

"This isn't the way to handle it," said the man. "There are a thousand other ways to—"

"No, there aren't."

A gust whipped past Lila behind her head, and the next time the woman spoke, it was from beside where the man's voice had just been.

"Do you want him to dispose of you?" she pressed. "He tried once already."

Lila stumbled, clutching the back of her head as Derek's coffee table flashed in front of her, replacing the momentary blackness.

His voice. I've heard it before.

She attempted to lower herself onto the sofa, but her legs gave way beneath her, and she crashed to the floor, one hand clutching the sofa cushion as the dark returned.

"Do you want to give him that chance, or do you want to be the one left standing? Damian won't give it a second thought, when he realizes what you are. Don't let him win."

Lila heard shifting beside her head, and then cold fingers lifted her eyelid. For an instant, she saw only the bright lights above her. When her eye focused, however, she caught a glimpse of dark hair, a sharp jaw, and lips set in a frown.

He released her eyelid, and it snapped shut, plunging her back into blindness.

Lila's scalp screamed as a hand lifted her head from the carpet by her hair.

"It wasn't me! It wasn't me, Ravenna!"

"What the hell do you mean, it wasn't you? There's recorded evidence! There's a video of you shooting him!"

Ravenna wrenched Lila's head backward, forcing her to look up. Ravenna was scowling, her teeth bared and her nostrils flaring.

"You don't have to do this, Lila," he said. "You don't have to—" He glanced over her shoulder, seeming to rethink the statement he had been about to make. "Just remember who you are. Remember who I—"

Lila squeezed the trigger. With a bang, the plasma bolt deployed into Damian's chest. His mouth hung open, prepared to frame words Lila would never hear. Pain creased his brow, and then his facial muscles relaxed, smoothing out as his eyes unfocused.

Tears streamed down Lila's cheeks, and she ordered her hands to drop the weapon.

Her thumb twitched.
She had to help him, had to stop the bleeding.
There's so much blood.
It seeped through his shirt, blooming like a poisonous rose across the pale green cotton.
Lila's feet refused to budge.
"You've done well," said Eddie's voice from behind her.
Eddie. Eddie was in the lab. Eddie did this to me. To Damian.
Lila ordered her feet to move. She had to face him.
He did this.
She needed to open her mouth, to make herself speak.
He made me kill—he made me—
Her jaw yielded to her command at last.
"What have I done?" Lila demanded. She whipped around to face Eddie, aiming the gun at his heart where he stood where the lobby met the corridor. "What have you done to me? Help him!" she screamed.
"You've done your part," he said. "Deactivate."

The room dissolved before her eyes as she collapsed.

"Please," Lila implored Ravenna. "Let me explain. I remember it all."

Ravenna watched her in silence for several moments. She let out a sigh so heavy her body seemed to deflate, and then she released Lila, who doubled over with her hands braced against the carpet as she struggled to catch her breath.

"Tell me. Now."

"Eddie. He reprogrammed me to attack Damian."

Silence filled the apartment.

When Ravenna did not move closer, Lila pulled herself up onto the sofa, where she struggled to catch her breath.

"Why would he do that? You expect me to believe you?"

"I don't know," said Lila, rubbing the back of her head.

"She said something about making sure Eddie was the last one standing, like Damian was going to come after him."

"She?"

As Lila replayed the woman's voice in her mind, she found it forming words she hadn't heard in her flashes of memory.

"I'm you. But better."

"An android," said Lila. "I don't know her name, but she attacked me at LDE. Said she'd known they should've gotten rid of me. I didn't know who 'they' was, but she was there with Eddie when he reprogramed me. I remember."

To Lila's right, the doorknob twisted, and she turned toward the sound as the door opened to allow Derek to enter. He stood on the threshold, wide-eyed, and then he appeared to revive from his stupor.

"What—?"

"We need to go," said Ravenna, cutting off Derek. "Now."

"Where? Lila, are you—?"

"We need to find Eddie," said Lila. "He made me do it, Derek. I remember everything."

TRAUMA

August 7, 2232

Desi eyed the slick chrome platform warily from behind the glass double-doors of the lobby where her brother had been murdered, and she did her best not to think about how close she stood to the spot where he'd taken his final breath. She had never occupied the podium in front of LDE's Manhattan office, but she'd seen far too many press conferences transmitted from it over the past few weeks for comfort.

You can do this, she told herself. *You owe it to him.*

"Are you all right, Miss Lawrence?"

Squaring her shoulders and lifting her chin, Desi looked to Captain Ryder, who stood beside another blue-uniformed officer just to the left of the doors. The captain's hair had gone a bit greyer since he'd been tasked with the murder case that had cost New York two of its three most famous robotics engineers and had still ended in a cold trail with the disappearance of the guilty parties.

With a nod and a tight smile, Desi shifted her attention to her surviving brother Derek, who stood on the podium in front of the building addressing a crowd of reporters. The bright flashes igniting every few seconds were, Desi knew, a bad sign. If the throng was this desperate to photograph her brother now, she couldn't begin to imagine how many flashes would blind her when she joined him on the podium in time with his announcement.

You can do this.

Derek looked out of place in a suit. He'd always been the one of the company's founders who'd taken his role the least seriously, at least in terms of dress. His heart had always been completely in his work, but he'd never wanted to be seen as a CEO. Desi recalled how often Derek had worn t-shirts while Damian, their elder brother, had been in black-tie attire and Eddie...

Desi stopped cold, determined to stop her thoughts from progressing any further, but it was too late. She already felt the strong arm wrapped around her chest, binding her arms to her sides. Her pulse accelerated so rapidly she had to swallow down the urge to throw up in her mouth. She took a few steps backward and clutched the nearest stable surface she could find—the security desk at the heart of the round, chrome-plated lobby. A shiver shot through her like an electric current.

She remembered sitting at a computer on the night of her brother's visitation service, watching the security footage of the night he'd fled for his life in this room. She'd watched as he'd vaulted over the desk and tried the front doors only to find the building on lockdown and his exit made impossible.

"Miss Lawrence?"

Desi's gaze skated over the spot where Damian had lain by the doors, bloody and broken after two shots to the chest, and to the police captain approaching her. She opened her mouth to respond, but the words died on her tongue at the sight of the captain's sidearm.

***

July 30

The warehouse was dim, lit only by lamps scattered throughout the bleak grey hallways. Desi knew the building hadn't been frequented over the last several years; since her brothers and Eddie had become successful enough to pay for high-tech labs within LDE's headquarters, they hadn't had much use for an additional space to store research and old projects.

As she turned a corner to the left, she caught sight of an open door. Her heart leapt into her throat, and she tightened her grip on the gun she'd stolen from beneath LDE's security desk.

She'd spent the entirety of the ride to the warehouse working to persuade herself that she was capable of killing someone.

He deserves it. He took you away and he tried to make Lila pay for it.

She still wasn't certain she could kill him.

As Desi reached the doorway, she slipped the weapon behind her back. She stepped inside to find Eddie digging through a stack of holofiles.

Her throat went dry, and her body turned to stone. The thought of the man who had wiped her tears and kissed gentle lines across her skin in the darkness being responsible for the death of her brother was unfathomable, now that she stood in Eddie's presence. Her hands shook so violently she feared he would hear the gun's mechanical parts quivering. She opened her mouth to speak and shut it again when no words would come.

He did this. All of it is on him. Be brave, Desi. Do it for Damian.

The thought of her brother falling backward into the glass front doors of the lobby was all she needed to summon her voice. It came out hard, like she'd swallowed a dagger that had finally worked its way back up her throat.

"Why did you kill him?"

Eddie froze so completely he might've been a statue.

"What are you talking about, Desi?"

"Why did you kill Damian?"

Slowly, Eddie laid his files on the table in front of him and turned to face her. His face was perfectly neutral apart from the furrow of his brow and the slight widening of his grey eyes.

"I don't know what you're talking about," Eddie said carefully. "Are you all right? Did something happen after I left?"

"What happened," Desi snarled, "is that I watched the security video." She pulled the gun from behind her back and trained it on his heart, willing her arms to remain perfectly still. "All of it."

"Desi, what are you—? Put that down. Please." With each word, his mask slipped a bit more, giving way to full-blown panic. "You're distressed. With what you've been through in the last week, I don't blame you for—Desi, please, put it—"

"Don't you dare call me that," she snapped, taking a step closer, moving across the threshold into the small office. Behind Eddie was a long glass window that overlooked an immense room filled with assembly equipment. Apart from the glass and the door Desi obstructed, there was no exit.

"Why? Tell me what's going on, Desi, I—"

"I swear." Another step, and only a few feet remained between them. "I want to know why."

"You know Lila shot him," said Eddie, shaking his head slowly. "You know she did."

"Lila wasn't in control of herself! You reprogrammed her to do it, to shoot him. You manipulated her! Just like you manipulated me."

At these words, his face fell, pain twisting his lips. "Everything I've ever told you about you and I is one hundred percent true. I have been in love with you since—"

"Stop it!" Desi shouted, needing to cut off the words that had sliced straight through her. "Stop! Tell me why you made her kill him!" She barely registered the tears sliding down her cheeks or the thought that she should've told Derek where she was. Raising her arms, she shifted the gun's aim to between his eyes.

"Because he was a threat!" Eddie cried, his face contorting in rage. "Everything I've ever done has been for this company. I've poured everything I am into it, and the one idea I wanted to pursue that he didn't—he was going to destroy me, Desi, and all that I've done, all that I've made. He was going to make sure I went down for every sin my creation ever committed, and she was made to help people, to take the place of humans in combat. I wanted to *save* lives, not take them! But he forced my hand."

"Lila isn't your creation." Desi's tone was low and venomous, her lips curling around every syllable.

"Not Lila. I—"

"Damian would never have turned on you because of some project! He would never have hurt you!"

Desi had been too consumed by her need to understand to realize that Eddie had moved just close enough to reach her weapon. In one fluid movement, he grabbed it by the barrel and pulled it to the side, but she refused to release her hold on the one advantage she still possessed. Eddie wrenched the gun back, and Desi, still clinging to it, found herself slammed hard into the edge of the table. Her breath exploded from her lungs in a huff as pain splintered up her side, but she clawed at Eddie's arms even as he dragged her farther onto the table. Holofiles clattered to the floor and splayed across the tiles, displaced by her body.

Don't let go. Don't let go.

Desi wrapped her leg around Eddie's arm and dug the heel of her shoe into his shoulder. Eddie hissed sharply.

"Enough!" he demanded. He removed one of his

hands from the gun to attempt to pry her foot away and remove her heel from where it dug into him, but she only pressed it in deeper. His grip on the gun faltered.

Using all her strength to pull the weapon back toward herself, Desi was unprepared for the sudden loss of resistance. She inadvertently squeezed the trigger, and the momentum with which she'd wrenched the gun toward her caused her to fall backward—with Eddie, whom the grip of her legs pulled along—through the glass the plasma bolt had just shattered.

***

August 7

"What are you doing?" she mouthed as she felt the ghost of a gun's cold barrel pressed to her right temple.

"I'm sorry."

She heard the words as clearly as though he were speaking them now. She heard the low tenor of the voice that had comforted her when she'd lost the brother that had been more like a father to her. The voice that had eulogized him with a touching speech about one fourth-grade boy befriending another and forging a lifelong bond that had been stolen away by murder. The voice that had whispered sweet words into her ear after she'd finally let down her guard enough to admit her brothers' best friend had meant more to her than a one-night stand and she'd allowed herself to fall for him again.

The voice that had whispered, *"This is not what I wanted,"* while the speaker had held a gun to her head.

***

July 30

Desi knew she was bleeding. She could feel the blood seeping through her dress and the bits of glass that had embedded in her skin on her impact with the window. What she'd anticipated would be a quick fall to the next room had turned into three-story tumble from the observation level to the floor of the immense assembly room below it. She was almost certain she'd imagined the tightening of Eddie's hands on her as they'd turned midair, Desi's stomach dropping sickeningly as she'd wondered exactly how far they would fall.

Eddie hit the ground first, Desi slamming on top of him on her side. The shards embedded in her left shoulder, when caught between their bodies, sank in deeper. She bit her inner cheek until she tasted the copper tang of blood.

Get the gun.

She vaguely processed that she'd let her grip loosen during the fall, and she reached out for the weapon with her eyes still closed. Her head pounded from the impact with the glass and with Eddie's shoulder upon landing, and when she opened her eyes, the room before her spun in a blurry wave of machinery and stacked dusty crates.

Beneath her, Eddie stirred. He let out a groan and searched the area with his hands, one skimming up Desi's back before he jolted and apparently regretted the sudden movement, as he let out a hiss.

"Are you all right?" he muttered.

Desi rolled off of him and attempted to stand, keeping her fingers locked around the gun's handle. Her legs quaked beneath her, and she knew her high heels would no longer serve her. She kicked them off and stumbled toward the stacks of crates at the heart of the room, determined to get far away from Eddie as quickly as she could. If he was still incapacitated, she had to use her moment of opportunity.

The warehouse swayed and dipped around her. Raising her free hand to the back of her head, she pulled her fingers away dappled with blood.

"Damn it," she said under her breath. She wound her way between a handful of stacks and leaned heavily against them, struggling to calm herself and remain perfectly silent.

She had no idea where Eddie was.

***

August 7

"Miss Lawrence."

The shipping crates that had materialized in her mind dissolved again to give way to the lobby and the concerned, mustached face of Captain Ryder.

"Are you all right?" he asked.

"I'm fine," she muttered.

"Are you sure? Maybe you should sit down." Ryder rested a hand on her shoulder, but she shook her head.

"No, thank you. He'll be ready for me any—"

As she spoke, Derek turned on the podium and stretched out a hand toward the lobby. Through the glass, he met Desi's eyes and offered her an encouraging smile.

"Thank you," she repeated to Ryder.

With a deep breath, she crossed the lobby to the doors and pushed them open. The quiet of the soundproof lobby was immediately drowned in a chorus of shouts for her attention and bursts of light from flashing cameras. She plastered on a smile and waved to the assembled reporters and the spectators clustered behind them.

"Today," said Derek into the microphone adjoined to the podium, "it's my pleasure to announce that I'm naming my sister Desdemona as LDE's co-president."

He took Desi's hand and gave it a reassuring squeeze, and for an instant, her smile grew more genuine. Despite the handful of robotics classes she'd taken in college, they had only been toward her minor and not her major. She held a bachelor's degree in theater, and she'd never felt that her brothers viewed her as qualified for even an entry-level position in the business they had begun with Eddie several years earlier.

She had no idea whether Derek really found her worthy or whether he simply needed someone he could trust in the position, now that one of the company's founders was dead and the other was a wanted fugitive.

"I'm thrilled to have her onboard," Derek continued, "and I know she'll be an asset to our team and to our brother's legacy." He inhaled deeply. "I believe we have time to take a few questions."

Desi's stomach lurched. She'd known this was a possibility depending on how long her brother spoke, but she was still unprepared for what the reporters could ask her.

A swarm of hands shot into the air. Derek called on a woman in the first row.

"Mr. Lawrence," the reporter began, "do you feel that your sister is qualified for such a demanding position, especially given the circumstances?"

"Yes, I do," said Derek flatly. "Next?"

Desi kept her focus on the edge of the platform upon which she and Derek stood, unwilling to meet the eyes of any of the people scrutinizing her.

"Have there been any new developments in the case pertaining to Eddie Dodson?"

Desi's hands clenched involuntarily into fists, her nails biting into her palms.

***

July 30

The ribbed metallic surface of the crate behind Desi's torso was both cool against her cuts and agonizing when it happened to bump the glass shards still protruding from her flesh. Her thoughts flicked to her phone, which she'd foolishly left in her purse in the floorboard of her car.

If I don't get out of here, I can't tell the police. I can't tell Derek or Lila—oh hell, Lila… She deserves for people to know the truth.

Desi pulled in a deep, shaky breath and took a step to

her left, peering around the crates to determine whether she was alone.

"It doesn't have to be this way."

The voice from behind her set her every hair on end. Even yesterday, it would have done the same without the accompanying lurch of her stomach.

How did he get so close so quickly?

Eddie's fingers closed around her wrist, and she stomped hard on his foot. He released her with a pained grunt, and she shot forward at as close to a dead run as she could manage when her every muscle and inch of skin burned and ached.

"Desi!"

At the sound of her brother's voice, she froze. She searched out the source of the sound and spotted Derek standing just inside a door halfway down the stadium-length room, and in an instant, she was charging for him.

"Derek! Run! It's Eddie, he's—"

Something slammed into her from behind so quickly and forcefully that she tumbled to the floor, the gun slipping from her grasp and sliding away from her as her head smacked against the concrete. The room spun sickeningly, and she fought to keep her eyes open despite the spots flashing through her line of vision as Eddie wrenched her to her feet.

"Let go of me!" Desi demanded.

Eddie kept one arm wrapped around her, pinning her arms to her sides, and forced her forward until they reached the gun. He retrieved it from the floor and pressed its ice-cold barrel to her temple.

"What are you doing?" she whispered, fear flooding through her limbs and turning them to stone.

"I'm sorry," he muttered. "This is not what I wanted."

In front of them, Derek had paused halfway to where they stood, his eyes wide and his shoulders heaving with his breath.

"Then don't do it."

"I have to, Desi. This is bigger than you know, and I won't be arrested." She felt him inhale, and when he spoke again, his voice was louder, reverberating against her back where it met his chest. "I need to get out of here, Derek. Let me leave, and I won't hurt her."

"Let her go!" Derek took a step toward them, and Eddie tightened his grip on Desi, pulling a gasp from her lips. "Why are you doing this? We've been nothing but good to you! How could you do this to us? To Damian?"

"Some things aren't about you," said Eddie.

He took a step backward, dragging Desi with him. She struggled against his grasp, but he dug the gun's barrel into her skin, and when the pressure and sting became unbearable, she abandoned her efforts. She kept her focus on Derek as she was pulled away from him, wanting nothing more than to reach out and throw her arms around him and apologize for everything she'd done. Blaming Lila, the company's first android creation, without looking for further proof, turning to Eddie in her time of despair instead of turning to her brother... Instead, she could only watch as he moved farther away from her.

***

August 7

"No," said Derek, "we know nothing new."

"Do you know where—?"

"No, we have no idea where he is. We have had no contact with him."

"Miss Lawrence, isn't it true that you engaged in a physical relationship with Dodson around the time of your brother's death?"

Desi's mouth went dry. She scanned the crowd at last, but with every eye fixed on her, she couldn't tell who had asked the question. The murmur of conversation had died, and beside her, Derek had frozen.

Desi knew no matter what she said, her words would

be misconstrued. She couldn't admit that she'd been involved with Eddie, because then what was to stop them from accusing her of being involved in Damian's death? She couldn't deny the relationship, because she knew some photograph or video clip would emerge that incriminated her and brought further damning scandal to the company.

"No comment," said Desi. The words tasted like ash in her mouth. She turned on her heel and started back toward the lobby, ignoring the shouts and flashes that followed her.

DUALITY

Eddie clung to the arms of his chair so tightly his knuckles were white. He watched Desi go on the telesense screen, her projected image seemingly just within the range of his fingertips if he only reached out to her. She was walking away from the reporter's question about whether she'd been in a relationship with him just as she'd walked away from him the morning after they had been together for the first time, and the sight made his chest ache.

He knew he'd given her reason to do far worse.

The moment she'd arrived in the warehouse carrying a gun, quaking head to toe, and demanding to know why he'd killed her brother, he'd lost everything. He'd only just persuaded her to give him another chance after she'd let her fear of sabotaging their friendship and his relationship with her brothers drive her to push him away, and he'd been the one she'd turned to after losing Damian.

Every bit of this is your fault, he reminded himself. *Every last piece of it.*

He stood between the computer and the operating table. Mia sat at the computer, her brown eyes narrowed, and the screen cast an eerie glow across her face as she sifted through files and memories. Eddie had briefly mentioned second thoughts about what they were planning, and Mia had demanded to be the one to ensure that Lila's memories remained gone.

Lila lay on the table, pale and unconscious, electrodes connected to each of her temples. Her cheeks were tear-streaked. At the sight of her, Eddie's knees weakened.

He'd never anticipated seeing his first creation in such a vulnerable position. He'd never intended her any harm.

"Mia, I don't—"

"It's done" said Mia flatly. She pushed back from the desk, and her chair bobbed where it hovered a few inches from the floor as she stood. She strode past Eddie on her way toward the table, giving his shoulder a squeeze that was too tight for comfort. "Too late."

Eddie recalled the first time he'd lain on the operating table within LDE's lab. Damian had been beside him, smiling encouragingly with a glint of determination in his eyes and assuring Eddie the first scan would be painless.

"After that... we'll do our best to keep it that way."

Eddie swallowed. He nodded stiffly and reminded himself of why he'd volunteered for this. Mia, the android he'd donated to the United States military to serve as a substitute for human soldiers and save lives, had inadvertently killed Damian's parents during a demonstration of her capabilities gone terribly wrong. The official report had said only that Henry and Samantha had been killed in a car accident in which a woman had run into the road and caused a van to swerve into their vehicle, but Eddie knew. He'd been there— he'd been watching her at West Point as she'd slaughtered the soldiers she'd been tasked with fighting, and when she'd fled the base, he'd followed her outside. But he'd been too late. By the time he'd reached her, the police had already been on the scene, and the parents of his two best friends and their sister had already been dead.

When Damian, distraught after the loss of his parents and

searching for solace, had suggested the company use its technology to find ways to preserve human life after death, Eddie had volunteered to serve as the test subject.

"Ready when you are," he said with an attempt at a smile.

Damian secured the electrodes attached to either side of Eddie's head, and then he moved toward the computer, where Derek sat.

"Close your eyes and try to clear your mind," said Damian.

A jolt of pain shot through Eddie's temple, and he raised his hand to brush the area. The headaches had grown more frequent since the night at the warehouse when he'd been faced with the fallout of his actions. He'd been shot in the knee, and he reasoned that he must've hit his head when he'd fallen to the concrete floor. He could think of no other reason for the splitting pain that now came to him more than once a day.

"Are you all right?"

Eddie blinked and looked up into the thin, pointed face of Mia. Her cropped auburn hair fell to her chin, and her lips were set in a frown.

For an instant, an image of her face contorted with rage flashed through his thoughts.

"You want to shut me down?" her cool alto demanded in his mind. *"For her?"*

As quickly as the image had come, it evaporated, and he was left with only the concerned Mia staring at him and the place where Desi had been standing a moment earlier on the telesense. Derek still stood at the podium, but Eddie couldn't focus on his words.

The headline at the bottom of the screen now read *"Desdemona Lawrence Refuses to Acknowledge Relationship with Brother's Killer."*

"Fine," Eddie told Mia. "Just a headache."

***

He stared at her where she sat slumped on the grey-carpeted living room floor, her hands pressed to the bleeding wound over the right side of her ribs. He tried hard to summon her face to the front of his mind as it had been not long earlier—she'd smiled as she'd lain beside him, her dark blond hair falling lazily over the edge of his pillow and brushing his shoulder. Each time he pictured her that way, the image held for only an instant before reality cracked through to reveal her here, her shirt soaked through with blood and her hands stained red.

"Desi?" he breathed.

Within the span of a heartbeat, he'd stood and started toward her, but before he could make it more than a step, Mia surged forward, placing herself between them.

"What the hell happened?" Eddie demanded, not bothering to hide the venom in his tone.

"Don't you realize she's a danger to us?" snapped Mia, her eyes narrowed and full of fire. "She knows about the Division. She knows they commissioned me, and she knows you went behind her brothers' backs to create me. She was going to the police, Eddie."

"You're insane," Desi muttered, shaking her head. "I wasn't going to tell anyone."

Eddie's stomach turned at the sight of the blood dappling her hair. He rounded on Mia, who took a step closer to him.

"Do you honestly believe her?" Mia pressed. "Do you really think she has any interest in telling you the truth, anymore?"

Eddie recalled the panic in which he'd turned Desi's attempt at retribution for her brother against her. When he'd realized they had no longer been alone in the warehouse, he'd taken the gun and held it to her temple, and though he never would've pulled the trigger, he couldn't expect her to know that.

He ignored Mia and brushed past her to Desi's side, crouching and laying a hand gently on her shoulder.

She wrenched away from his touch, hissing and clutching at her side as the movement upset her wound. It was all Eddie could do not to wince at her determination to escape him.

"What did she do to you?" he whispered.

"You mean besides causing the accident that killed my parents and helping you murder Damian?" Desi snarled. "Get away from me."

Eddie swallowed and stood.

"She's a liability," said Mia flatly.

"What do you want, Mia? What are you suggesting?" Eddie stared at her, studying the hard, brown eyes he'd designed in a much simpler time. He'd been determined to help the Division bring the United States out of a military slump and save the lives of needlessly endangered soldiers, but Mia had never been his answer. From her first trial, when she'd fled the Division's base at West Point and initiated the traffic incident that had killed Henry and Samantha Lawrence, she'd been nothing short of a plague.

"We need to protect ourselves," she said simply.

In a blur of auburn, she flew from the living room, returning seconds later with a sleek silver plasma gun in her hand.

"She knows too much, Eddie." Mia raised the gun and took aim at Desi's chest.

"Mia, put it down. Put it down, *now.*"

Eddie stepped toward her, his hands raised as his heart pounded sickeningly, feeling as though it were creeping its way up his throat. He spared a glance in Desi's direction to find her staring at the gun, her lips set firmly.

She won't beg Mia to stop. I think she'd welcome it, at this point.

The thought sickened Eddie. What had he done to her? To the woman he loved?

Mia tightened her grip on the gun, and Eddie was certain she would pull the trigger. He willed himself to move more quickly than he'd ever moved before, and in an instant, he stood between Mia and Desi, inches from the barrel of the gun.

Mia's eyes widened. As she watched him, Eddie understood everything he'd tried to block from his mind. He felt the ghost of Mia's fingers wrapped around his throat, and he remembered.

"You want to shut me down? For her*?" she snapped.*

Eddie pulled at her fingers, struggling to pry them from his neck, and he could only splutter and clutch at her as she lifted him just slightly and his feet lost their purchase on the warehouse floor. Her grip tightened.

"You—are—dangerous," Eddie choked.

"Whose fault is that?" Mia cried, her arm trembling. "I'm what you made me," she continued. "And you're supposed to love *me."*

Eddie attempted once more to speak, but he found himself unable to force words past the burning in his lungs. He surrendered, allowing his eyes to close.

He was only vaguely aware of the world around him as he was lowered carefully to the floor.

"Maybe the other you will," Mia whispered.

"I couldn't have moved that quickly," said Eddie, refusing to shift his focus from Mia's face.

"You're imagining things," said Mia with a tight shake of her head.

"No, I'm not."

Eddie reached for Mia's wrist and wrenched it to the side, and when she yielded with a sharp exhale, triumph washed over him along with a deluge of sadness.

"When did you replace me?" he hissed. "When I brought you out of storage to kill you?"

"You're delusional. And I don't want to hurt you, so let me go."

"What did you do to the other me? The—"

The next word died in Eddie's throat. He knew this was the truth his mind had been railing against, the secret that had come to him in flashes after he'd hit his head in the fight with Desi at the warehouse. He knew he couldn't deny it any longer, now that he knew he was strong enough to restrain Mia, fast enough to outmaneuver her.

He remembered programming the copy of himself he and the Lawrence brothers had christened E-2. He remembered the synthetic blood they'd poured into the copy's metallic veins and the extensive tests through which they'd replicated his own body, and he remembered when he'd chosen to shut Mia down permanently. When she'd decided that perhaps she could persuade his copy to love her.

"What did you do with the real one?" he whispered.

Mia's eyes narrowed. "You are real, Eddie. Every bit of you. You're standing here with a very real choice, and you have the chance to make the right one, this time."

She wrenched her arm free and darted to the side, and as she retrained her weapon on Desi and squeezed the trigger, Eddie charged forward, throwing himself between them.

He felt the insurmountable burning of the plasma bolt as it sank into his chest, and he dropped to his knees. His eyes lost their focus on Mia, though he heard her scream, and after a moment, he abandoned his efforts to remain upright. He fell backward, half-processing the blood spilling from his chest and spreading warmth over him as it seeped outward along his shirt. He tasted liquid iron.

We did a damn good job designing it, didn't we?

He didn't want to spend more than an instant wondering if he could count himself among those creators.

He searched the room as well as he could without lifting his head, and he saw that Desi had managed to stand. She was staring at him, mouth open, visibly horrified.

"This is *your* fault!" Mia cried.

Eddie returned his focus to her as she raised the gun again. For the first time since her creation, he saw a tear sliding down her cheek.

"Put—it—down," said Eddie as he fought back the bloody cough he could feel rising in his lungs. "It won't—solve—anything."

Slowly, Mia lowered the gun. She crouched beside Eddie, laying the weapon beside him as she leaned over him, laid her head on his shoulder, and wept.

"I'm sorry. I didn't mean to—"

"I know."

Eddie wrapped his arm around Mia's back, hoping she understood the gesture as a comfort as he held her in place. He stretched the fingers of his free hand out over the soft grey carpet and wrapped them around the grip of the gun. He held her close as he pressed the barrel to her back and fired.

Mia convulsed once and collapsed heavily on top of Eddie. She was still.

He let out a long breath and shifted her off of him, and she landed on the floor with a thud, staring unblinkingly up at the ceiling.

He dropped the gun to the floor beside Mia and looked to Desi, who had taken a step toward him while he'd been looking elsewhere.

"She would have killed you," he said softly.

"I know."

At last, Eddie could hold back his coughs no longer. He spluttered and fought against the blood pooling in his throat, but he couldn't keep himself from coughing up some of it. Desi flinched as she watched him.

I don't want her to see me like this. So weak.

"I'll call an ambulance," said Desi.

"No. Please, just—just stay with me."

Slowly, she moved to his side and sat beside him. Her blue eyes shone with unshed tears. He supposed she didn't want to allow herself to weep for him, and he couldn't blame her even an ounce.

"I'm sorry she hurt you," said Eddie. When she nodded stiffly, he continued. "And I'm... sorry for everything I've done to cause you pain."

At last, a tear broke free and slid down Desi's cheek.

"We could've..." She swallowed. "We could've been happy."

Eddie felt the sting of tears at the edges of his own eyes, and within a few seconds, Desi was blurry where she sat beside him.

"I'm sorry," he muttered. "So sorry. For all of it."

The real Eddie wouldn't have done this to you, he thought, but he couldn't allow himself to speak the words. If she knew what he was, that he was just a flawed copy that had succumbed too easily to Mia's manipulation, she would leave him here to bleed to death alone.

"I don't expect you to forgive me," he said. "I could never ask that of you. Just know that... I never wanted to hurt you."

"Okay," she said with a small nod.

Eddie paused and studied her. One hand still held the wound Mia had given her, and he looked to the other.

"May I?" he asked. "Just once?"

She reached out and gave his hand the smallest of squeezes.

"Thank you," he said. "And I want you to have this." With his free hand, he reached into his pocket and withdrew his LDE keycard, passing it to her. She released his hand just long enough to set it beside her. "Go to the warehouse. You can use that to open the only locked door. You'll... understand."

The edges of his vision had begun to darken. He succumbed to another round of coughs, this one more ragged than the last. When it subsided, he spoke once more.

"I know you don't feel it, Desi, but... I love you."

He felt her grip on his hand tighten, and then his limbs

were too numb to feel. He struggled for breath as the darkness overtook his vision, and then he saw nothing.

***

Desi stared blankly at the white curtain separating her from the hospital's other patients. She was feeling incredibly out of place, surrounded by worried doctors on the curtain's other side and her brother, who was still talking from the chair beside her bed even though she had stopped listening several minutes earlier.

For the duration of the trip to the emergency room, Desi had distanced herself from those around her, unable to speak as she and the paramedics had moved farther away from the man she had once loved. The sight of Eddie there, on the floor, had been too much to bear. After calling Derek to come to her aid, she had resigned herself to the corner, where she had become little more than a shell, no longer connected to her own mind or anything around her. She'd made half an attempt at explaining the situation to the paramedics and to Derek, and she had barely uttered a word since.

Eddie had been a liar. A murderer. A monster. So why did she ache with her every fiber, now that he was gone? Had she really been honest with herself when she had decided that she felt nothing more for him?

It's too late, Desi. It's too late.

He had killed her brother, but he had died for her.

"...got out as quickly as we could, when they attacked. We still haven't heard anything from Rachel or Andrew, and as soon as you're discharged, we need to get on the road. We can't take the chance on Osiris figuring out where we are."

When Derek stopped speaking, Desi blinked and returned her focus to his face at last. He'd already explained to her everything he knew of the Division and its secrets, including Mia's hand in the deaths of their parents, which she hadn't had enough strength left to admit she'd already known. Her ability to process the attack he'd described was nonexistent, at the moment, and she barely registered the sting left over from the lasers used to seal the wound just above her ribs. The doctors' orders to remain here and "take it easy" were nearly forgotten.

The keycard in the pocket of the pants she had draped over the chair beside Derek's called to her, demanding her attention.

"Go to the warehouse. You can use that to open the only locked door."

Eddie's words echoed through her head, taunting her. What could have possibly been important enough to him to lead him to spend his last moments giving her the key? What was behind that door?

The need to know ate at Desi until she could stand it no longer.

She knew Derek would not approve of her investigating. Overprotective as he was, he would want to find out the truth for himself before allowing her to be put in another potentially dangerous situation, and he certainly wouldn't want her following a trail set by Eddie.

But the key had been meant for her, and she had to know.

"I'm sorry you went through all that," she said at last. "I... Derek, I need to use the restroom. I'll be back soon."

She sat up, and the pain in her ribs knocked the wind from her newly healed lungs. Derek moved to help her, but she slapped at his arm.

"I'm fine."

"No, you aren't."

Desi ignored him. She pushed herself to her feet and slipped on her shoes, closing the distance to the chair as quickly as she could.

"What are you looking for?" he questioned as she rifled through her pants pockets.

"My phone," she lied, slipping the keycard surreptitiously into the pocket of her gown before turning to face her brother. "It's not here. It must have fallen out in my car."

"When you're feeling better, after we regroup with the others, we can find your car and see if the phone survived the crash. Lila and Ravenna should be back from the cafeteria soon. We'll talk to the doctors and see how long they think you need to stay."

She nodded vaguely and then threw her arms around Derek's neck, embracing him.

"Thank you. For coming to find me, I mean, and for bringing me here. I love you."

"I love you, too," he said, surprise evident in his voice.

"But I'm fine," she asserted. As she spoke, she gently grasped the key ring protruding from Derek's pocket and withdrew it. She paused for a moment, and when she was satisfied that he hadn't noticed, she took a step backward. "I'll be back."

She smiled and slipped through the curtain without another word, moving at a brisk walk until she had cleared the emergency room doors. Desi then broke into a run, nearly bumping into several people as she wove through the halls of the hospital. She flew out the front doors and into the dark parking lot, where she retraced her steps to Derek's car.

The road zoomed past her in a blur as she drove toward the place she had visited only once before, on one of the most traumatizing nights of her life. But that evening in July could not hold a candle to the one she now found herself hurtling through.

When she arrived, she found the concrete warehouse's perimeter covered with yellow police tape. Without hesitation, Desi slipped through the tape and into the building.

She stumbled through the darkness for what felt like hours before emerging, at last, into the immense room where she had once been held at gunpoint. Her breath shaky and anything but even, Desi scanned the walls for a door.

There.

In the far corner, concealed almost entirely by the long metal staircase that rose to the observation deck.

She jogged toward the door, ignoring her burning lungs, and paused for only the length of a heartbeat before producing the card.

"I came," she whispered as she scanned it through the panel set into the wall. "I don't know why, but I did."

The red light on the panel beside the door turned green, and the door slid open.

Lights flickered on to reveal what looked like a small laboratory, much like the one at LDE. Frowning, Desi stepped into the room, and the door sealed itself behind her. Apart from a single silver table to her left, the only item present was a chamber set into the back wall. It was covered by a glass dome, which appeared to have frosted over. She crossed the room silently to stand beside it, observing. There was a control panel nearby, and at its center, she spotted a green button marked "Release."

I've come this far, Desi told herself. *Might as well go all in.*

She pressed the button.

Air hissed from either side of the dome, and slowly, the frost faded. Beyond the glass was a figure that became clearer with each passing second.

"No."

Coughs sounded from the other side, mingling with deep breaths, gasps for air. Finally, the glass dome shifted to the right and slid back into the wall, revealing the figure within.

"Desdemona?"

The all-too-familiar grey eyes met hers, and she couldn't breathe. She couldn't think.

This isn't real.

Trembling, Desi began to back away from the sight

before her. Had she not just witnessed Eddie's death? How could he be in front of her, struggling to catch his breath and working to steady himself as he took a shaky step away from the chamber?

She sank to the floor, staring blankly ahead, unable to focus. *This is impossible. This can't be happening. He's dead. He's dead.*

Slowly and unsteadily, Eddie lowered himself to the floor beside her, concern etched into each line of his face.

"This isn't real," she breathed.

"What do you mean? What happened to you? Are you hurt?"

Desi let out a clipped laugh at the absurdity of his questions. She glanced down at her hospital gown and then returned her focus to his face, to the lips she'd kissed more times than she wanted to admit to herself.

"I'm going insane."

"I don't think that's true," said Eddie, shaking his head. "Please, tell me what's wrong."

His eyes were filled to the brim with sincerity.

Either by some twist of fate he really has no idea, or he's a better liar than I thought. And that… would be saying something. She took a deep breath, but the words she forced herself to say came out as scarcely a whisper.

"You're dead."

CONVERGENCE

Derek glanced sideways at Lila as he maneuvered through the streets of Highland Falls. Her golden-blond hair was pulled back from her face, allowing him to see her eyes, which were a lighter blue than anyone else's that he had ever seen.

Lila happened to meet his gaze, and she smiled, a gesture which he returned without pause.

He was beginning to worry.

He'd allowed himself to indulge the way he felt about her briefly when he'd persuaded himself to seek her out and protect her from the accusations surrounding his brother's death, but now that she was no longer in immediate danger, he'd tried his best to avoid any thoughts that might lead to acknowledging what he feared was true.

He couldn't allow himself to love her.

Could he?

The morality of android-human relationships had been called into question before courts over the last few decades, but most of those courts had refused to pass judgments that could be considered legislation on the matter. The only case Derek knew of that had found a human at fault for filing a marriage certificate with an android had centered on an early Genesis model—an Eve, if he recalled correctly. The android's programming hadn't been sufficiently advanced for the court to rule that she held enough autonomy to make her own choices, at least not choices of that caliber. But Lila had been an advancement in technology the likes of which the world had never seen before her. She was, as the media had heralded her, "*the world's first near-human android.*" Her thoughts were her own, her feelings were her own, and...

Derek realized he had no idea how she felt about him. He'd never asked her, and he had no idea whether it was wise to do so. If she didn't love him, would she have any desire to continue working with him, after he admitted something like that? Or would his admission strain their relationship to the point of breaking?

"It's the one on the right up here."

Ravenna's voice from the back seat pulled Derek rather abruptly into the present, and his focus flicked out the front windshield to the house in question.

It was small and off-white, with green shutters and a picket fence. Derek knew immediately that the house was old, as it wasn't made of metal the way most buildings had been for the last century.

"You're sure?"

"Of course I am," said Ravenna impatiently.

Derek pulled the car up to the curb in front of the house and parked it. He, Lila, and Ravenna filed out and gathered on the passenger side, standing close together, each apparently waiting for one of the others to be the first to speak.

"After you," said Derek finally, looking at Ravenna.

She took a deep breath and gave a stiff nod, squaring her shoulders and striding to the gate at the center of the fence. She unhooked the latch and opened the gate, leading the way up the path to the house.

As he followed Ravenna toward the building, Derek felt something brush against his fingers. He looked down to see that it was Lila's hand, and electricity crackled up his arm at her touch. She gave his hand a quick squeeze, which he returned before she retracted hers.

Ravenna hesitated at the door.

"It'll be fine," Lila assured her. "She's your aunt. She'll tell you the truth."

"That's what I'm afraid of."

She knocked on the door, and they waited in silence.

There was a scuffling from within, followed by what sounded like footsteps nearing the group.

"Who is it?"

Ravenna cleared her throat. "Aunt Clarisse, it's Ravenna."

A small pause followed, and then the sound of a latch, and the door opened. The woman on the other side had dark brown hair that was greying at its roots, and her hazel eyes searched Derek and Lila warily. When her focus landed on Ravenna, whom she resembled strongly despite the difference in their ages, her expression softened.

"They're my friends."

The woman Derek assumed to be Clarisse frowned slightly, glanced behind the group, and then addressed them. "Come in. Quickly."

They did as she bade them, stepping into the small sitting room at the front of the house. The room was cluttered, with books and newspapers and holofiles covering what space the green-and-white furniture did not.

Derek heard Clarisse close and lock the door behind them. She ushered them farther inside, waving them to the sofa. Somewhat uncertainly, Derek sat down, with Lila to his left and Ravenna on her other side. Clarisse sat across from them in an armchair.

"It's been so long," she said to Ravenna with an expression that suggested that she still hadn't fully come to accept that her niece was actually sitting in the room with her. "Why now?"

"We need your help."

Derek turned to Ravenna, who looked somewhat guilty upon admitting that this was her reason for visiting.

Clarisse frowned. "What could I help you with? You're not in any sort of trouble, are you?"

"No, no," said Ravenna quickly. "It's not like that. We've come to talk to you about... the Division."

Clarisse blanched. She broke eye contact with Ravenna, looking instead down at her own folded hands in her lap.

"How do you know that name?"

Derek drew a deep breath. "It was mentioned in an e-mail you sent to Edward Dodson," he said. "Regarding the android Mia."

Clarisse continued to stare at her hands. "It's classified."

"Please, Aunt Clarisse. We need your help. It's urgent."

The elder Mitchell sighed. She looked up, and her eyes fell on Derek. "I know you. You're Derek Lawrence. And you—" She turned to Lila. "—you're the first LDE android."

Lila nodded slowly.

"To this day," said Clarisse, "we have no idea how they managed to perfect you. We tried so hard and for so long... We've lost so much."

Ravenna frowned. Derek exchanged a glance with Lila before returning his focus to Clarisse when she spoke again.

"It was during the Middle Eastern War. Human error caused so much pain and destruction. We needed a way to win the war, and our soldiers were dropping like flies. President Hartley had an idea—an idea that should have worked. We should have succeeded."

"So..." Lila hesitated. "Why didn't you?"

"What we were trying to do had never been attempted. We had no idea where to begin, when she told us to create the perfect soldier. One that would obey without question. An android."

Derek listened, both entranced and horrified. He

couldn't imagine one of LDE's androids being turned into a soldier and ordered to kill on command.

A flash of Eddie suggesting they create a model for use by the military passed through his mind, and he squashed it.

"The Division—the Perfect Soldier Division—was created to accomplish this. We assembled a team of the top minds in robotics at the time, hoping that, together, they could achieve the goal. Soon, a group of seven androids was created. They were exactly what we wanted: soldiers to the core. They fought perfectly in all our tests. We deployed them to take out a small band of enemy forces that had taken refuge in Dahab."

There was a long silence.

"What happened?" asked Lila.

"They couldn't find the enemy group. So... they tore the town apart. They killed *everyone*."

Lila gasped. Ravenna closed her eyes and sighed.

"My God," said Derek quietly.

"Needless to say," Clarisse plowed on, "the androids were decommissioned. We did our best to keep the situation quiet, but somehow the media got ahold of it, and our cover was almost blown. Several other Division officials and I decided to wait it out in Canada until the fever died down."

Ravenna dropped her head into her hands. "We believed you," she muttered.

Her aunt addressed her. "What was that?"

Ravenna looked up, her features set in a blend of disbelief and indignation. "We believed you when you said you had nothing to do with it. Mom, Dad, Bryce, me. We defended you to everyone—to our own family, to the reporters that came snooping. We lied to all of them. Bryce defended you until the day he died."

Clarisse's face fell. "Ravenna, I never meant for any of it to happen. I never wanted you to have to lie for me. But there was nothing I could do, I—"

"You could have told us." Ravenna stood, folding her arms across her chest. "We still would have lied to everyone else to protect you, but at least we would've known what was really going on."

"I couldn't," Clarisse said weakly. "I couldn't put you in danger like that."

"And look where we are now! Trying to figure out why you were working on something in secret with the man who killed my fiancé!"

There was silence. Clarisse turned her gaze to the floor.

"Ravenna, calm down," said Derek. "That's not going to get us anywhere."

She ignored him. "How did Eddie get involved?"

Clarisse sighed. "While we were out of the country, some of the scientists continued their research. They tried to fix the androids, to perfect them. It never worked. Eventually, the others and I returned to the U.S. When the conflict with China began, the Division saw an opportunity to prove that they could finally succeed. But they needed help. Your company was in the news all the time." She inclined her head to Derek. "I recognized your names—yours, your brother's, and Edward's, I mean. I remembered hearing from Ravenna's father that she had friends interested in robotics when you were all in high school."

Derek shot Ravenna a look. Apparently, her aunt was unaware that she had inadvertently sparked that interest when her niece had borrowed a file on androids from her desk drawer.

"We began… 'paying attention' to your company. We decided that of the three of you, Edward was the most likely to sympathize with our intentions. I approached him about designing something for the Division. We met again later, and he said he had run the idea by you and Damian."

Derek nodded vaguely. In the corner of his vision, he saw Lila tense.

"You didn't approve. However, Edward still wanted to

help us. So he created Mia. She seemed like everything we had hoped for. But... we were wrong. She had no conscience, no remorse. Like the androids the Division scientists created, she just destroyed. We tested her at our installation at West Point, and during her trial, four people were killed."

By this time, his face was set in a deep frown. It was not the revelation that Mia had killed that disturbed him, but that this had all occurred at West Point. Only a few blocks outside the Military Academy, his parents' fateful accident had taken place

"Then she ran. She left the building and took off through the streets. Derek, I..." Clarisse trailed off, but he didn't need to hear anything more. He already knew.

His lungs felt as though they were on fire, and he couldn't stop the choked sound that burst from his throat.

Lila grabbed his hand.

"What's wrong?"

Ravenna turned toward him, concern visible in her eyes. She glanced from him to her aunt and back again.

A long moment passed before he was able to speak. He squeezed Lila's hand tightly, hoping that holding onto her would lessen the pain, but it did not.

"Mia killed my parents."

***

"Derek?" Lila asked the darkness.

She lay on the sofa in Clarisse's living room, her eyes open and strained against the black night. She had found herself unable to sleep, and her mind reeled with the wealth of new information she had become privy to over the last few hours.

After explaining her role in Mia's creation, Clarisse had made dinner for Lila, Derek, and Ravenna, and then she had decided to allow them to spend the night. Ravenna was somewhere else in the house in a guest bedroom, and

Derek had taken the living room's recliner.

He had kept Lila in the dark. Why hadn't he mentioned Eddie's military proposal? Was she not an integral part of the company, and had she not deserved to know? She tried to convince herself that Derek had simply never thought about the idea again after Eddie had suggested it, at least until Clarisse's email had surfaced. Nevertheless, doubt had crept into her mind. Was she truly trusted?

"Lila?" Derek sounded half-asleep, and she immediately regretted addressing him, at least until morning.

"How...?" She trailed off with a frown. She wondered how best to broach the subject that she knew was highly difficult for him to discuss. Since the accident had occurred, Lila had done her best to refrain from mentioning it. "How did you know what Clarisse was going to say, earlier? About your parents?"

She heard him sigh.

"I don't know. I guess some part of me always knew there was something wrong with the story I was told about it. Someone ran out in front of a van, and the driver swerved to avoid hitting her. He hit my parents' car, and..." He paused. "The driver gave a description of the woman he was trying not to run into, but no one ever found her. That shouldn't have been possible. My dad was a senator—they launched a full investigation and everything. And Eddie seemed to change completely after it happened. I suppose it was guilt. I should've known. I should've done something."

"It's not your fault," Lila asserted. "Even if you had figured it out then, what would you have done?"

"I don't know. I really don't."

There was a loud knock at the front door.

Lila jumped. She heard movement in the room and then felt Derek standing beside the sofa. She sat up and glanced down the hall, wondering whether their hostess had heard.

"Clarisse?"

The voice from outside was female, and it sounded desperate.

"Clarisse, it's Blue Team! Let us in!"

Hurried footsteps drew near, and the living room was bathed in light. Lila squinted. Her vision adjusted quickly, and she saw that Clarisse had entered the room and was headed toward the front door. Behind her, Ravenna made her way down the hall at a much slower pace, one hand rubbing her eyes and the other resting on her stomach. She looked quite pale.

Clarisse unlocked the door and opened it. She stepped out of the way, allowing a small group of people to rush in, and then locked the door behind them again.

A woman with red hair stood at the front, looking out of breath and supporting another woman with dark skin and a wasp tattooed on the side of her neck. Behind them stood a bearded man carrying an unconscious woman with a white-blond ponytail.

"We didn't know where else to go," said the redhead.

Clarisse's expression could've belonged to someone who had just seen a ghost.

"No, it's fine," she said faintly. "What happened? What's wrong with Charlie?" She indicated the unconscious woman. "Set her down, Lex, over here."

Clarisse waved them over to the sofa. Lila leapt to her feet to give them room, and the man called Lex placed Charlie where Lila had been a moment earlier.

"We thought we could handle it," said the tattooed woman in an undertone. "We were so *stupid.*"

"Handle what, Casey?" Clarisse looked desperate, now.

Utterly confused, Lila moved closer to Derek. He slid an arm around her and watched the newcomers warily.

"Our mission," said Casey. "Our target. Mia."

Lila tensed as Casey knelt beside Charlie and took her pulse at her neck.

"Are you Division?"

All conscious eyes fell on Ravenna, who lingered at the edge of the room. She did not falter under their gaze, though she still didn't look entirely well. The redhead frowned and looked from Ravenna to Clarisse and back. Clarisse sighed heavily.

"I didn't have a choice," she said. "They already knew about Mia. They needed to know the rest of the story."

The redhead took a deep breath. "Rachel won't like this."

Clarisse laughed shortly. "Your cousin has more important matters to deal with, by the look of the four of you."

"She's out, Kat," said Casey. "That's not good." She lowered her voice and whispered to Charlie. "You're not allowed to die on me, Blondie." She leaned close and kissed Charlie's cheek.

"Try to wake her up, if you can," said Kat. "She may have hit her head."

"Mia threw her down a flight of stairs," Lex explained as Casey shook Charlie's shoulder. "We went to Dodson's house to look for anything that might connect him to us, and we hoped we'd run into the android. We got our wish."

"Why would you want to see her?" Lila asked, unable to keep herself quiet any longer.

Kat and Clarisse exchanged a glance, and Kat sighed.

"I guess it won't hurt to tell you, considering how much you already know. We're the team that's supposed to be taking her down, and she's outmaneuvered us at every turn."

"Don't take it personally," said Lila with a shake of her head. "She's good at that."

"It seems we have a lot to talk about," said Kat. "And, Clarisse, there's something you should know. She said she's coming for us. All of us. You're in danger."

Silence hung thick in the air for several moments, and then Clarisse sighed.

"What do you want me to do?"

"We're on our way to West Point," said Kat. "I think you should come with us." She paused and looked from Lila and Derek to Ravenna and back to Clarisse. "All of you."

Lila met Derek's eyes and then Ravenna's, and after each of them had nodded, she followed suit. She knew their greatest chance of safety came with staying together, and if that meant merging their small group with this set of Division agents, she knew it improved their odds exponentially.

"I resigned," said Clarisse. "I'm not part of the Division anymore."

"But you were when all of this started," said Lex. "You commissioned her. I'm sorry, but she has more reason to harm you than any of us. That's why you need to come."

Clarisse smiled bitterly. "And you really think you can protect me, if she wants me dead?"

"Go with them," said Ravenna. When Clarisse turned to her with a raised brow, she continued. "Don't be ridiculous. If she's after you, it's the only option."

"Fine," said Clarisse after a beat. "Let's go."

Kat inclined her head appreciatively to Ravenna. "We'll have to take two cars."

"Mine's outside," offered Derek.

"All right. Let's move quickly."

Lex lifted Charlie from the sofa, and everyone filed out onto the lawn, Clarisse shutting the door behind her when she exited. As they walked, Lila watched Kat glance over her shoulder several times on the way to where the agents' black car was parked behind Derek's.

"Not how I expected tonight would go," Ravenna mumbled from Lila's left.

"At least we're getting answers," Lila replied.

Ravenna let out a flat laugh. "The farther we get," she said, "the more I regret asking the questions in the first place."

***

Derek jumped as the high-pitched wail of the sirens assaulted his ears. His eyes wide, he turned to Lila, whose mouth hung open in an unspoken question. They had not yet reached the rooms they had been allotted at West Point when red lights had started to flash along the tops of the slate-grey walls.

They had arrived in the middle of the night, and less than twelve hours later, the world was imploding around them.

Derek surveyed the corridor. All around them, people began to run in every direction. Shoulders bumped Derek's and hands shoved him out of the way as West Point went mad.

Lila slid close to him, taking his arm. "What's going on?" she called over the din.

He shook his head through what felt like ten feet of water, unable to focus or think. He had no idea what could possibly have triggered the alarm other than a catastrophe the likes of which he was thoroughly unprepared to face.

"I have no idea," he called back to Lila. "Let's find out."

They took off at a run. Their footfalls were drowned out by the sirens and the shouts of the people around them.

A bang resounded through the hall.

Derek and Lila dove to the floor as the sound of concrete crashing into itself followed, and he pulled her close on reflex. Countless others had also flung themselves down in fear, their eyes searching for the source of the sound.

An enormous hole had appeared in the wall at the end of the hall Derek and Lila had just come from. A man and woman walked through the hole and the rubble surrounding it, their faces cold and pale in contrast with the woman's vibrant red hair and lips.

"Have you missed us?" called the man over the wail of the sirens. "We're home."

Derek's heart lurched. The blast hadn't seemed like that of a bomb—it looked like the pair of newcomers had caused it.

Androids.

He didn't recognize them, and he knew that none of LDE's androids had been designed to destroy.

The ones the Division created. They didn't decommission them. Is Mia with them?

Fear surged through him, and he pulled Lila to her feet. "Come on. We have to find Ravenna and get out of here."

A second bang sounded, and Derek froze. He knew this sound. It was one that he had become far too familiar with over the last few weeks to be able to ignore. He glanced over his shoulder at the gunshot in time to see that the red-haired woman had raised her fist to catch the shot. She opened it to reveal a plasma burn.

"Run!" Lila breathed, her voice hitching on the word.

Derek sprinted forward, away from the newcomers and the shots that filled the air. Barely a second passed before the screaming began.

From the corner of his eye, Derek saw Lila turn her head toward the noise.

"Don't look back," he said. "Just keep going."

They thundered through the complex, and Derek was certain his stomach would roil its way out of his body. He hadn't been this frightened since the night he'd followed Lila's recently recovered memory to the warehouse to square off with his best friend.

A man in a military uniform flew through the air in front of them, crashing into the wall with a sickening crack.

"This way!" shouted Lila, pulling Derek in the opposite direction of where the man had come from. Though his every fiber screamed at him not to, he chanced a glance down the other branch of the hallway.

Another pair of androids was tearing their way through a crowd of people, snapping necks and weapons with equal ease. The two were brown-skinned, the man's complexion a few shades darker than the woman's.

"*Where is she?*" the woman cried.

Derek wrenched his focus from the androids and poured all of his concentration into where he and Lila were running.

"Who do you think they're talking about?" Lila's voice was forcedly calm, though Derek knew her well enough to sense the terror beneath the surface.

"I don't know," he said.

In that moment, he felt utterly useless. He couldn't hope to fight the androids without a gun, and he doubted he would be able to pause long enough to search out one that hadn't been broken or crushed beneath rubble along with its owner. Lila possessed incredible strength and speed, and yet she was fighting her nature to remain with him, even at the cost of her own life.

In that moment, he knew he had to tell her.

"Lila, there's something I need you to know."

She looked at him then, her face a composite of alarm and incredulity. "Derek, I don't think now is really the best—"

"Please. Please let me speak," he implored. "If something happens, I will have lost my only chance."

She nodded slowly, glancing between him and the overcrowded, overloud hall, which lost structural integrity by the second as more crashes and bangs filtered in from all sides and smoke poured through the air.

"Go ahead," she said.

"I love you," said Derek. "I have for longer than I can remember, but I've been denying it because I—" A blast from behind the pair sent them flying forward and crashing to the hard metal floor. Derek gritted his teeth against the pain of his shoulder slamming into the surface and pushed himself up again as Lila did the same beside him, and they ran. "I shouldn't have waited this long."

Shrieking, a group of suited people plowed their way between Derek and Lila as they ran in the opposite direction. Panic coursed through him until she reappeared at his side.

"Derek, I—"

"Go on," said a smooth female voice from behind Derek.

His heart jumped into his throat.

He turned to see the female android he'd just witnessed breaking soldiers' necks standing inches from him. Her irises were bright emerald, and they didn't look remotely as human as those belonging to LDE's creations.

"I'm interested to see where this goes," she said, raising a brow.

"Don't play with them, Bastet."

The dark-skinned man had appeared at her side, and he was scowling. He reached out and grabbed Derek by the throat.

Gasping and spluttering, Derek struggled to pry the man's fingers free. An instant later, Lila stood between him and his attacker. She twisted the man's arm until he released his hold on Derek and rounded on her, his eyes—mirrors of his companion's—wide with shock.

"One of us?" he asked, a hint of amusement coloring his tone.

As Derek rubbed at his aching throat and backed toward the wall, Lila scoffed.

"Not even close," she said.

The woman called Bastet charged at her and grabbed her by the shoulder, slamming her hard against the wall.

"You'll wish you were," she snarled.

Lila drove her fist hard into Bastet's stomach, sending her flying backward into the wall a few feet from where Derek stood. Lila hissed, and Derek realized a moment too late that Bastet had swiped at her at the moment of impact and left four deep scratches across Lila's clavicle.

Synthetic blood pooled along the lines and dappled the ripped cloth of her shirt.

Bastet took a step toward Lila, glaring daggers.

"Why them over us?" she asked. "What can they give you?"

The sound of gunfire from the right drew Derek's attention once again, and he looked up as Bastet deflected a plasma bolt into the wall. She locked eyes with her companion.

"Anubis," she said simply.

Without further discussion, the two of them charged toward their attackers in a blur, and Derek watched in horror as they intersected a group of men and women in camouflage partially obscured by the smoke pouring down the hall.

A round of fire followed instantly, intermingled with screams. A few moments later, smoke was all Derek could see from the direction where the androids had gone.

"This way, come on!"

Derek's head whipped toward the voice. Kat stood a few yards down to his left, looking flushed and furious. Behind her stood Casey, Charlie, and Lex, their guns trained on the direction the androids had gone.

Lights began to dance around the edges of Derek's vision. He had nearly begun to question his physical state and his sanity when he processed how pungent the smell of smoke had become.

He took another glance down the hallway to his right, and his fears were confirmed.

West Point was ablaze. Flames leapt along the walls, consuming everything in their path.

"Where's Ravenna?" Lila cried, grabbing Derek's hand.

"Outside with Abigail," called Kat, "waiting for us."

Immense relief crashed over Derek. At least one person he cared for was safe.

"What about Rachel?" This, too, came from Lila.

Kat was silent for a long moment. "I think she got out. She and Andrew were going to find Rachel's mother."

"They'll be okay, Kat," insisted Lex. "They're both trained and both smart. They'll be fine."

Kat nodded. She did not, however, appear convinced.

"There!" yelled Casey. "Through that door!"

Despite his exhaustion, Derek pushed himself forward. He could not stop running if they were to survive. He felt suspended in time, moving forward in a circle, unable to gain ground. His grip on Lila's hand was the only thing keeping him from falling over the edge. The group reached the door. Derek and Kat rammed into it, but the only result was the pain that splintered up and down Derek's arm from the point of contact.

"Got it."

Lex stepped to the side and took aim at the door. He deployed a series of shots into its frame until he'd blasted it off its hinges, and then with a strong kick, he knocked it free. It crashed to the ground outside.

"Let's move," he said.

As the blaze engulfed the remainder of the hallway, Derek, Lila, and the unit known as Blue Team fled.

VESSEL

It was dark. At first, that was all Rachel knew. The feeling hadn't returned to her limbs—the oppressive numbness that she had come to call her reality held her immobile and threatened to pull her from consciousness once again.

Footsteps hurried toward her, and she wanted to turn away from them, to find some way to escape before they reached her. Her eyes ached, and she knew that if she could see her reflection, she would find mascara trails tracing her cheeks.

She hadn't given them the satisfaction of hearing her scream.

Light exploded around her now, and her hands moved on reflex toward her eyes, but brown leather wrist restraints held them firmly in place. The pain in her eyes multiplied a hundredfold as the light assaulted them, and she closed them in refusal to acknowledge whoever had entered the room.

"Well, she's alive," said the voice of Isis flatly.

"That's a step in the right direction." Rachel knew this voice belonged to Bastet, who sounded farther away from her than Isis had. "It's better than we hoped."

A hand closed firmly around Rachel's wrist. "Open

your eyes. Now."

When she did not immediately oblige, Isis tightened her grip on Rachel's arm. Pain surged outward from the place the android gripped, and at last, Rachel surrendered.

She opened her eyes to find the blond, sharp-chinned Isis standing over her where she lay on the table at the center of the concrete room. The dark-skinned Bastet lingered a few paces behind, watching the encounter with hesitation. Rachel had no idea whether Bastet had been programmed with the ability to feel remorse or whether the android was simply wary of getting too close to the captive daughter of the president who had commissioned her.

Isis leaned forward, lowering her angular face to examine Rachel, who held Isis's gaze steadily, her hatred simmering just beneath the surface. She believed Isis saw it there. The android smirked and turned to her counterpart.

"Come look at her eyes."

Bastet gave a small nod and closed the distance between herself and the table. She stopped beside Isis and looked down at Rachel. Bastet's frighteningly bright emerald eyes widened, and she looked from Rachel to Isis and back again.

"Does this mean it worked?"

Before Isis could answer, a sharp, pained cry sounded from outside. The androids exchanged glances and moved in a blur of motion out the door.

Rachel was left alone, the sound of her breathing her only company. After several seconds of unbearable quiet, shouts burst from another room.

"How could you let this happen?"
"Don't you dare blame me!"
"We took care of Hartley! This was your job!"
"There was nothing she could have done!"

Another sharp cry followed, longer than the first and full of agony. The shouted argument subsided immediately, the voices Rachel recognized as belonging to

Isis, Hathor, Bastet, and Horus giving way to the pain of another, which was also familiar. Rachel's weary mind processed at last what it had failed to grasp after the voice's first cry.

"*Andrew!*" Rachel struggled violently against her restraints for freedom. "*Andrew!*" The tight leather straps began to give, and her resolve doubled as the idea of freedom became slightly less impossible.

"No, Horus, leave her. She isn't a threat. Not yet, anyway."

"If she realizes what she can do, she will b—"

"Hathor, shut him up. She can hear, now, remember?"

"We're losing him," said Bastet in a small voice.

Rachel wept, her breathing shallow from her struggle. Biting her cheek to suffocate the strained yell that wanted to burst from her lungs, she wrenched her arms upward, pulling the restraints free of the table. She stared at the leather cuffs encircling her wrists and the snapped metal links that had held them in place.

In the other room, the androids had fallen silent.

They already know I'm trying to get free. And they have Andrew. What more can they take from me?

With this thought at the front of her mind, Rachel sat up quickly and bent forward to find her ankles similarly restrained. She grasped the straps and pulled at them with all her strength, and they gave much more easily than the first pair had. The force she exerted on them was greater than necessary, and they flew from her hands and over her shoulders, thumping to the floor behind the table.

Trembling, Rachel stood.

Why was that so easy? I shouldn't have been able to do that.

"Wait a second, come back here, he's—damn it, Horus, we lost him."

Rachel's heart sank, leaden, to the pit of her stomach. Her fear evaporated instantly, and she burst from the room toward the voices.

The air was heavy with an old, dry smell Rachel

couldn't place. Her eyes adjusted rapidly to the darkness of the tunnel, much to her confusion, and she processed the sight of a track laid into the ground that seemed to move in an endless straight line. She followed the track and a light several yards down to her left, and they led her to a cracked door. She gave it a small push, and it swung open.

Andrew lay unmoving on a perfect double of the table Rachel had just occupied. Hathor was bent over him, one of her hands entwined with Horus's. The latter was a few steps closer to the door than the former, as though he had been on his way out. Bastet stood on Andrew's other side, her hand closed around his wrist as though she had been checking his pulse. Isis stood at the foot of the table, watching the others with half-concealed sadness.

Why do they look like they care about him?

Before another thought could pass through Rachel's mind, Horus whipped toward her.

"Not to be rude, love," he said to Hathor, "but I told you so."

Hathor stiffened and stretched to her full height, turning to face Rachel with a question in her cold emerald eyes. Her red lips were pressed together in firm calculation. She took a step forward, which Rachel mirrored with a step backward.

"There's no point in trying to run," said Horus flatly. His sharp nose and narrowed eyes gave him the look of a predatory bird preparing to strike. "You won't get far."

"Then why do you all seem so afraid of what I know?" Rachel's eyes flicked from Horus to Andrew, and she was unable to hold herself back any longer. She launched forward, pushing past Horus and Hathor and ignoring the red flags raised in her mind by how easily they were moved by her shoves.

She flung herself down at Andrew's side, kneeling and leaning over him to examine his pale face. She laid her shaking hand on his cold cheek. A terrible sob ripped its way from her lungs, and she dropped her head onto his chest and closed her eyes.

"How could you do this to him?"

"We tried to save—"

"Hathor." Isis cut her off with a stiff shake of her head.

"To answer your question, Ms. Hartley," said a voice from behind Rachel, "killing is what we were built to do."

She did not look up; she knew that if she turned, she would find Osiris. The sound of footsteps followed his words, and he entered Rachel's line of sight when he stopped beside Isis. He met Rachel's eyes, and he faltered for only the slightest fraction of an instant. Then he spoke again with a cool calm that was unnerving as she sat weeping over Andrew's body.

"We followed orders," said Osiris, "when we were born. I suppose you could say our flaw was that we followed them too well. It was doing what the Division told us that led to our downfall. We received an order to end a threat, and we succeeded. We also managed to ensure that the threat would have no way to begin again. But that wasn't good enough for them. No, they saw only that we had killed. That we had taken the lives of more humans than they intended. Do you know who gave us the order to kill, Rachel?"

She did not answer. She held his gaze evenly through her tears, trying not to stare at the jagged scar tracing from his left temple to the corner of his mouth.

It seemed the Division's creations had all fallen into the same trap. She recalled the day she'd taken over the organization, when she'd learned about Mia, the android robotics mogul Eddie Dodson had created for the Division after Osiris and the rest of his line had failed. Mia had been responsible for countless deaths even before she'd participated in the highly publicized murder of Damian Lawrence.

Like Ra, one of the original seven androids commissioned by Rachel's mother, Mia had since been killed. Unfortunately, six remained.

"No?" Osiris pressed. "It was your mother, Isabella. And Clarisse. They told us to kill, and we did. They created us, you see. We were everything they wanted and more. But then they didn't want us. We were too good at what we were created to do. And do you know what else the Division did? Of course you do. It wasn't under your watch—Clarisse was still running the farce of an organization when they attacked—but you've picked up the pieces nicely over the last several years. They had the nerve to try to slaughter us. And we will not allow Ra's death to go unpunished."

He looked up, then, away from her. His hate-filled green eyes roved from one android to the next, and Rachel noticed then that Anubis had entered the room.

"*You've taken your revenge!*" she shouted. "You've picked off the assassins one by one, and you've burned West Point to the ground! What more do you want?"

Osiris smiled darkly and shook his head. "Yes, we have. Most of the assassins are dead. However, Ravenna Mitchell lives, and she is the one responsible for Ra. The others were unimportant collateral damage."

Rachel leapt to her feet and rushed toward Osiris. In a flash, Horus and Hathor grabbed her arms and pulled her backward. "Andrew is not 'unimportant collateral damage,'" she spat venomously. "I loved him!"

Osiris smirked at her from the end of the table. Beside him, Isis watched Rachel with a measured reproach.

"There's the fire we're looking for," said Osiris, nodding his approval.

With an enraged cry, Rachel wrenched her left arm forward, dragging Hathor with it. The android flew through the air and landed with a *THUD* atop a startled, livid Horus. Rachel took a step toward the pair at Andrew's feet.

"Stop her." Osiris's tone was uninterested, but his eyes were intrigued.

Suddenly, pain splintered through the back of Rachel's

head where Anubis had stricken her, and the room swam before her eyes. She slipped to her knees and then fell forward, catching herself against the cold concrete with her palms and unsteady arms.

The blurry outline of Osiris moved toward her. When he spoke, it was as though he were addressing her from the other end of a long, dark tunnel.

"You'll be too good at your job, too. I'm counting on it."

Her arms quaked and gave in to the strain, and she fell to the floor.

"You're going to save us."

The room spun a final time, and the blurred figures of the six androids and the man Rachel loved faded into darkness.

***

"How long do you think she's going to be out like this?"

"God knows what they did to her. I can't begin to guess. It could be days."

"Can we afford to stay here that long?"

"If we have to move her again, so be it. But for now, I'd like to keep her as comfortable as possible."

The voices surrounded Rachel in her state of mental incoherence. The ache that had plagued her eyes the last time she'd awoken had settled into a dull pressure, and though she remembered being bludgeoned into unconsciousness by Anubis, the blow had left her no residual pain.

Where am I? she wanted to scream. *What have they done to me?*

Her thoughts were several steps behind the world around her, and the voices had ceased to speak by the time she registered to whom they belonged. It was not the androids—her captors—who surrounded her now.

She recognized several of these people. The first voice

belonged to Clarisse, and the second belonged to Rachel's cousin, Kat. Rachel did not know who the third speaker was, but if Kat and Clarisse were with him, he could be no danger to her.

Summoning all of her strength and willpower, Rachel sought her voice. This perpetual fog in which she found her mind yet again infuriated her. It kept her weak.

Weakness was something Rachel had never tolerated in herself. She had always needed to be strong for the sake of those around her. When her father had died, her mother had needed her to be strong enough for the both of them, even though Isabella had been president at the time. Living confined to her wheelchair after a failed assassination attempt following her second term had drained enough of Isabella's passion for life on its own, and when it had so closely followed the accident that had stolen her husband during that term, the strain had been almost too much for her to bear. Rachel knew that without her, her mother would not have made it through those dark final years in office and the ones that had followed.

She now understood why.

A deep ache filled her chest as she recalled who else had been present in the tunnel, and a tear slipped down her cheek.

"Andrew," she muttered.

"Kat, she's awake!"

The abrupt sound of approaching footsteps startled Rachel. A cold hand touched her face, and she breathed in deeply to keep herself calm. She had never been so easily put on edge.

"Rachel, can you hear me? It's Kat. Wake up, please."

Rachel forced her eyes to open, and the pain in them sharpened again as they dilated in the light. A group of people shifted into focus above Rachel, and she steadily surveyed them.

Her cousin was leaning over her with worry etched into every line of her face. As Rachel watched, however, relief cracked the pain in Kat's expression and a smile crept onto her lips.

"Thank God. I was afraid we'd lost you."

Rachel replied with a vague attempt at a laugh. Clarisse sat on the edge of the bed on which Rachel found herself, and she was watching Rachel carefully. Beside Kat stood Ben McNaire, the son of Isabella Hartley's successor to the presidency, whose mouth smiled though his eyes were terribly sad.

"What did I miss?" Rachel croaked.

Kat laughed tightly. "I'm not sure where to start."

Ben glanced at his watch. "I would advise waiting until it's light out, which is in about three hours. For now, making Rachel comfortable and assessing the damage they inflicted on her should be the priority. On the subject of comfort, Kat, is it all right with you if I head next door and turn in? It's... been a long night."

Kat nodded solemnly. "Of course, Ben. If you need anything at all, you know where we'll be."

Ben nodded and turned away, slipping out the door and closing it behind him. After a long moment, Kat returned her attention to Rachel.

"His mother is dead. Isis killed her on a live broadcast."

Tears stung Rachel's eyes. "I guess that means things have gotten worse since I went out."

Kat sighed heavily. "You have no idea."

***

Rachel stumbled toward the dresser, her head both swimming and pounding until spots surged through her field of vision, roiling over the backdrop of the hotel room and creating their own incoherent masterpiece in its place.

The color green flashed in front of her, blinding her. She was vaguely aware of losing her balance, falling into the dresser and knocking over the water-filled glasses she and Kat had used with their last meal. Other objects slipped beneath her hands as she collapsed, but she did not identify them. She landed on the carpet with a thud, and the world was filled with white noise.

Hands pulled at her, lifting her. Endless moments passed in this limbo, and then she felt cushion beneath her. The pain slowly began to ebb away, and Rachel forced her eyes open.

She lay in her bed, her friends standing beside her and looking positively petrified. Kat turned away to speak to Clarisse, and Ravenna, Clarisse's niece and the one Osiris sought above all others, laid a hand over her forehead.

Ravenna studied her with a deep frown. When she met Rachel's gaze, however, she looked as though the floor had dropped out from beneath her. By this time, Kat had returned her focus to the two of them, and she watched Ravenna with an arched brow.

"What is it?"

Ravenna blinked, and there was a long pause.

"Nothing," she said at last.

Kat frowned. She appeared to disregard whatever had just transpired as she addressed Rachel, taking her hand. "What happened, Rach? We were outside, and we heard a crash. When we came in, you were on the floor."

Rachel attempted to shake her head, but the effort brought a fresh wave of pain. She closed her eyes and inhaled deeply before focusing on Kat again.

"It's just a headache. I'll be okay."

"Most headaches don't make people pass out," said Ravenna.

"I didn't pass out." Rachel's words were certain, but her tone was far from it. Truthfully, she was unsure of what had happened to leave her lying on the carpet facing unbearable pain and the unshakable image of green light.

Green light. Green.

At that moment, Ben hurtled into the room. He was visibly anxious, and his breathing was shallow, as though he had been running.

"Turn on the telesense."

Clarisse frowned. "Ben, what's going—?"

"All I can say is that it's probably not a bad thing everyone is in here. Splitting up from this point forward could be disastrous."

He grabbed the remote from the dresser and turned on the telesense set into the wall across from Rachel's bed. Projected from the screen was an image of a reporter Rachel did not recognize but the text projected over her image identified as Anukit.

"—rewards of three million dollars per person, no questions asked. Lord Osiris has not disclosed their specific crimes, only that they are heinous and treasonous."

"What is this about?" breathed Rachel.

"Keep watching," Ben replied.

"For those of you just joining us," continued Anukit, "I will repeat the offer Lord Osiris has made. He has put forth the sum of three million dollars for the apprehension of each of the following people: Derek Lawrence, Edward Dodson, Desdemona Lawrence, and Ravenna Mitchell. He requests them alive. If you have any knowledge of the whereabouts of these people, contact—"

Ben turned off the telesense.

"Lord Osiris?" asked Rachel.

"His control is growing by the day," said Clarisse. "I'm surprised he hasn't found us already."

***

Pain spread through the back of Rachel's head as she was slammed into the wall of what had once been her mother's office. The fingers wrapped around her throat made breathing next to impossible, and her weapon lay discarded across the room and out of reach.

Clarisse had advised her against joining the mission to rescue Eddie Dodson and Desdemona Lawrence from

Osiris, but Rachel had insisted, and the plan had gone more terribly than she could've imagined.

She stared into the eyes she had so often seen on the telesense in the months since July and for the last several years since their owner had become famous. Their brown was disrupted and degraded by jagged bolts of emerald green, and Rachel knew what that must mean.

What scared her more than the fact that Damian Lawrence had been recreated as a bastardized android copy and was trying to kill her was the fact that she had seen precisely that shade of green in her own eyes.

It had appeared first behind her eyelids when she had felt the world slipping from her grasp and oblivion had prepared to claim her. That ominous emerald had then resurfaced in her reflection. It had been so fleeting and so sporadic that Rachel had convinced herself that the loss of Andrew and her months in solitude had finally shattered what had been left of her sanity and led her to see things that could not be.

She had known from the beginning, though, that her mind was not playing tricks on her. There was a reality hidden within those flashes of emerald that Rachel would rather die than face; concealed behind the headaches and fits of nausea and inexplicable fainting spells and depression that had plagued her since her abduction was a terrible truth that she did not understand or accept.

She gasped as the copy of Damian that called itself Set squeezed her throat, constricting her windpipe until she began to feel she would slip away into nothingness at any second.

"We had such hope for you," said Set, and his hard expression seemed to cover genuine disappointment and loss. "It wasn't supposed to end like this."

"Then—don't—let—it."

Rachel found speaking nearly impossible, and she knew that she would most likely be unable to force any more words from her lungs, which felt as though they were ablaze. She closed her eyes, prepared never to open them again, and prayed silently that her mother and her friends would remain safe.

A knife slipped into the base of her skull.

She screamed. The pain was so intense that it took Rachel several moments to realize that nothing had actually pierced the skin but that the agony was spreading from within her. Roaring filled her ears, raging and insurmountable. She felt far away from her body and from her mind, locked away in some distant part of herself that was too separate to be called Rachel. She fell through the air, and when she landed on the carpet, she realized that she had been dropped by Set.

Tossing and writhing over the floor and digging unsuccessfully at whatever had set the torture in motion at the back of her head, Rachel became unaware of the rest of the world. She knew only the darkness that pulled her in totally until she could feel no more.

***

Mia stood near the center of the room, holding the gun responsible for the plasma wound in the chest of her only companion as a tear ran down her cheek.

"Put—it—down. It won't—solve—anything."

She lowered the weapon, too traumatized by what she had just done to care that she was letting Desdemona—who stood near the door on the other side of Eddie, who was bleeding on the floor—live. Mia set the gun on the floor and rushed to Eddie's side, leaning over him and crying into his shoulder.

"I'm sorry," she said. "I didn't mean to—"

"I know." He wrapped an arm around her, and for just a moment, she felt that she had been forgiven. All of her sins, all of her faults, were understood and unjudged.

Then she felt the agony surging through her chest and back, and she understood betrayal. For the first time, she knew what it was to both love and hate. This lasted only an instant, as in the next, she was dead.

She had loved him. Mia had never thought herself capable of love, and she would sooner die again than admit it to another, but she had allowed herself this one human emotion.

And what did it do? It killed me.

"Mia?"

She opened her eyes and stared up into the face of Osiris. A smirk slid onto his lips.

"I was beginning to wonder if you'd ever wake up."

She sat up quickly, ignoring the vertigo that swam through her head, and pushed herself to her feet.

"You should hold st—"

"I've been still for too long," she said with a shake of her head.

She moved as quickly as she could for the mirror across the room, and Rachel Hartley's face greeted her in the glass, her dark green irises interrupted by crisscrossing emerald lines. Mia raised a cautious hand to her cheek, and in the mirror, Rachel did the same. As Mia smiled, she watched the lips of the Division's leader twist upward.

"We didn't succeed with Ra," said Osiris. "It killed him and Andrew when we tried to implant him."

"We don't need Ra," said Mia, turning to face him as excitement pulsed through her veins. "We'll be fine on our own."

GODDESS

Hathor leaned against the railing with a practiced ease as her synthetic fingernails drummed a steady pulse against the metal.

She detested waiting. Why should she be made to wait for anyone, least of all a human?

"Which one of you was it?"

The voice came from behind and above her, from the top of the stairwell. Light filtered down the flight of steps from the door that led to the ground level and out of the decrepit tunnels Hathor's associates had taken to using to conceal their work. A moment of silence passed in which the human must have realized that Hathor had no intention of speaking with the door open, and a sigh echoed down the steps.

The door closed with a bang. Footsteps approached her in the darkness, and then he was at her side.

"Which one of you killed him?"

Hathor inhaled deeply at the voice of Harry Masters, former Division assassin and her current informant.

"Don't you think you're better off not knowing?"

A thoughtful pause followed. "Probably," Harry said at last.

She smirked. She knew the human spoke of the human President Ethan McNaire. He didn't need to know which android had shot the man or which had finished the job in the hospital.

"How long until the next phase begins?"

"Patience," she said curtly. "Justice cannot be rushed."

"You might be interested to know that Hartley lied to you. Seward's team is not in Washington."

"What?" Hathor demanded. Her eyes narrowed, and her nails bit into her palm.

"Don't worry," said Harry patiently. "I've got it under control. I convinced Beck to assign them to guard the new president. They're on the way here, now."

Hathor let out a quick, relieved breath. Hartley and her lies would be dealt with, but at least the plan had only been delayed and not derailed. "Good," she said. "Osiris will be pleased to hear it. You continue to earn your place in our new order, my love."

Hands sought her out in the darkness and pulled her into an embrace.

"How long will we meet like this? How long will we live a lie?"

"The time for the truth is coming," she said, her tone reassuring. "I can't promise when it will be here, but it's coming."

"I trust you," said Harry. "That's good enough for me."

The instant he'd finished speaking, she felt the brush of his lips against hers. Barely an instant later, a loud crash from farther down the tunnel caused him to leap backward.

"Go," she muttered. "We will meet soon."

Without another word, he started up the stairs. Light bathed the area once more and then disappeared along with the sound of his footsteps as the door closed.

"You know," Hathor mumbled into the darkness, "for someone who is in on the plan, it's obvious how much you don't want me to do my part in it."

"I know the role you have to play," said her mate as he appeared beside her, "but that doesn't mean I have to like it."

"Please, Horus." Hathor rolled her eyes. "You know you have nothing to fear. You know I have no more interest in the human than I do in knitting."

"But you play the part so well."

"Of course I do. It's the part I was created for. I was named for the goddess of love, remember?"

Horus grunted noncommittally. "Just remember what you're going to have to do, when the time comes. Our new order is no place for traitors."

Hathor's face fell, and she was glad the darkness obscured her. Yes, she knew what she would have to do. It had been part of the plan from the beginning. Then, she'd held no qualms with it. The human had betrayed the Division and his orders to kill Hathor, and he could never be fully trusted. But now... The double meaning of Horus's words was not lost on her.

If she turned her back on the plan their leader had devised, she would be the one without a place in the new order.

***

Hathor pulled tight the bandage she'd wrapped around Harry's wounded leg. Harry winced in pain, and Hathor bit her lip.

"Hold still. I just have to tie it, now." When she'd done so, she sat back on her haunches and watched as he closed his eyes and inhaled steadily. "You'll be fine, Harry. It's a flesh wound."

"Yes, a flesh wound inflicted by Osiris."

Hathor sighed, pursing her lips. "He's just disappointed. Believe me, if he was really angry with you, you'd know. Either that or you'd be dead."

They sat in one of the White House parlors, Harry on the edge of the sofa and Hathor on her knees on the rug on the floor. She was no doctor, but she knew enough about anatomy to know that Osiris's shot had not been intended to permanently handicap Harry. It was a punishment, but not one that would last.

So far, the plan had gone almost flawlessly. Osiris had led the strike on the human capital and seized it for his own base of operations, and the only snag had come in the form of Hathor's informant, who had been responsible for ensuring a particular Division task force was led out of the way.

Harry pushed himself to his feet, gritting his teeth in visible agitation. Hathor stood to help steady him, but he waved her off with a shake of his head.

"I didn't lie to him. You know that. Seward's team was outside. How did Osiris feel when the bodies were identified and he realized he'd killed the wrong team?"

Hathor shrugged weakly. "He wasn't happy. It didn't really matter that the other team was dead. They weren't our main targets, but they were part of the Division. Killing them affected the other side, but it wasn't as devastating a move as we needed to break them apart completely. I don't think he blames you. Not now."

"Good to know."

Without another word, Harry stormed from the room. Hathor stared after him for several long moments before sinking with a groan onto the sofa.

Even when we win, I lose, she thought. The relative peace surrounding her since the successful execution of the plan to scatter the members of the government organization that had created her and then sought her destruction had allowed her time to pause and evaluate herself. Though she was an excellent actress and would continue to play the part of loving Harry, her heart truly belonged to Horus. They were created for one another, two halves of one being. Without him, she had no idea who she would be or what her purpose was. Though they had been programmed to feel something for one another, it was what had occurred between them in the years since their birth that had become this deep love she knew could not be entirely credited to their creators. They'd been united against the creators who had turned on them—united against the world.

Since that fateful day when Harry had been assigned to kill her by the Division and decided not to go through with it, Hathor had taken a liking to him that was difficult to explain. She'd tried to convince herself that she had only begun to believe her own lies, but she knew it was more than that. As much as she tried to think that she could never feel anything but hate for a human, she knew that was untrue. She didn't love Harry, but she had come to view him as a friend, and friends were not a luxury she could typically afford. The other androids were all she had ever known, apart from killing.

Truthfully, some small part of her mind had begun to question what she was. If she'd acknowledged that one human was good for something other than cannon fodder, what of the rest of them?

Enough, Hathor, she chastised herself. *You're not allowed to think that. You were created for one purpose: to destroy. The Division's enemies, at first, but you were too good at that to be allowed to continue. And now what have you destroyed?*

Her eyes stung. For the first time in her life, she was faced with a feeling of sickening emptiness she could not explain. A terrible trail of water had begun to trickle from the corners of her eyes. Was this what it felt like to cry?

Why would they add this to my programming?

She leapt to her feet and wiped furiously at her face, unwilling to accept this weakness. She was better than this, better than human. She was perfection. She was exactly what the Division had made her.

If what it had made her was a monster, that wasn't her fault.

***

Fools, she thought. *All of them.*

At the sound of the scream from the hallway, Hathor moved at the top speed her physiology allowed toward the noise. She found the captives Osiris had used to draw out their Division colleagues a few yards from where she'd emerged. Desdemona seemed to be unconscious, cradled against the chest of Edward, who was clearly attempting to seem more composed than he felt, as the poorly bandaged cuts he'd sustained from Osiris's interrogation had begun to bleed again. Beside them stood an agent Hathor didn't recognize, who was staring at a body on the floor wearing a Division uniform, and Kat Seward, the head of the task force Harry had been entrusted with dispatching.

They could've gotten away, if they weren't so fragile.

It was then that Hathor recognized the dark hair and permanently resigned expression of the fifth member of the group.

Clarisse Mitchell, the Division's founder. The woman responsible for Hathor's creation. The one who should've fought to protect her and her kind but who had, instead, turned assassins on them when they couldn't be adequately controlled.

Hathor had no time to react before Horus was at her side. He moved in a blur to stand beside Clarisse, gripping her wrists and twisting until she dropped her gun.

"Hello, Mother." Horus smiled, his pointed features made sharper by the uneven light of the chandelier above him. "It's nice to see you."

Pushing away her feelings of betrayal with a shake of her head, Hathor rushed to stand beside Kat. She grabbed the agent's arm and twisted it backward, effectively disarming her and slipping the plasma gun she'd recovered into her own jacket pocket. She held Kat's arm firmly in place and spoke to Clarisse, wishing Osiris's plan didn't restrict her from harming the woman, who he believed still possessed too much valuable information to risk.

"We're allowing you to live, Clarisse," said Hathor. "Be grateful."

"Why? So I can watch you destroy the world?"

A shout of Horus's name from a room down the hall arrested his attention and Hathor's, and after exchanging a glance, both of them nodded.

"Take care of them," said Horus with a nod to the humans. He pulled Clarisse along with him as he strode away down the hall.

"Where is he taking her?" demanded the male agent Hathor didn't recognize. "Why are you keeping her here, if you're not going to hurt her?"

"I said we're letting her live," said Hathor flatly. "That's not the same thing as not hurting her." She returned her focus, at last, to where Edward stood. Her eyes lingered on his for a moment and then drifted to Desdemona, and her mouth pressed into a thin line as she saw how pale the woman had become. Hathor knew firsthand how cruel her leader's methods could be, and she worked hard to push the twist of regret away before she could think on it too heavily. "That one doesn't seem to have much time left."

Edward opened his mouth, but before he could speak, Desdemona lifted her head slightly.

"I wonder which of you will be next," she said, her voice strained.

Hathor took a step toward her, maintaining her grip on the agent all the while, and Edward stepped backward. Desdemona let out a pained hiss, and her eyelids fluttered. Edward glanced down at her before returning his focus to Hathor.

"Please," he insisted. "Please, let us go."

The android stopped in her tracks, her nose crinkled, and her brows drawn. "Why in the world would you expect me to do that?"

"If Horus were in danger, wouldn't you do anything in

your power to keep him safe?"

The android's expression slid back into carefully guarded neutrality. "What does that have to do with anything? Horus is perfectly fine."

"But if he weren't?" Eddie challenged. "Would you lay down your life for him?"

Hathor simply stared at him.

I would. Of course I would.

"Eddie," mumbled Desdemona, "what are you doing?"

He did not answer her. Instead, he continued to speak to Hathor.

"I would like to make a request."

Hathor responded with a tight laugh but said nothing, continuing to watch him curiously.

"Take me. Keep me here, do what you like with me—kill me, I don't care. But let Kat and Beck take Desi out of here. If you let them go, I will do whatever you ask."

Desdemona frowned and opened her mouth, presumably to protest, but he squeezed her shoulder.

Hathor blinked.

It was clear to her how deeply these two humans felt for one another. She'd only begun to understand how their kind worked, but even so, she could imagine Harry making a similar plea for her life. *Horus... of course he would, wouldn't he?*

Hathor turned away from the humans and pulled in a long breath.

"Go," she ordered.

The corridor was perfectly still.

"Get out of here!"

At her shout, the humans started toward the front doors. Hathor ignored the thanks Edward called to her and lowered her head into her hands.

***

"Has she given you any trouble?"

At the sound of Osiris's voice from outside the door, Hathor gripped the sheets so tightly she heard the material rip.

I knew I shouldn't have let them go. But how was I supposed to know he'd turn on me?

"She hasn't said a word since you left."

The door opened, and Hathor caught sight of several guards standing outside as Osiris entered. His eyes were the same emerald as her own—the same color she'd seen reflected back every time she looked at Horus, who she knew was now being similarly held in a room a few doors down the corridor.

Hathor kept her jaw set obstinately and her brows raised in an unspoken challenge to Osiris's authority as she sat at the edge of the bed in the room she'd been locked in since he'd found out she'd allowed the humans to leave.

"Would you like to explain your actions?" The threat in his words was unconcealed.

"Not particularly, no. I don't believe they require explanation."

Osiris shifted his weight and began again. "What could possibly have driven you to let the humans leave when you were under orders to execute them if they attempted to escape?"

At this, Hathor allowed her façade to fall away completely. She launched herself from the bed and moved in a blur to stand inches away from Osiris, not bothering to hide her fury.

"What purpose would their deaths have served? Edward could have proven useful to you. The girl could have been your best bargaining chip, if any situation required one, and if there's anything I've learned, it's that any leverage one can have over the enemy is worth whatever it costs to keep it. Keeping them would have cost you nothing. Killing them, however, would have eliminated whatever sway you held over the Division."

Osiris seemed to consider her words for a long

moment, and then he smiled. Hathor blinked and frowned, certain this couldn't bode well.

"I almost believed you," Osiris said. "I suspect you've been formulating that little explanation since they left, and I'll admit, it was very convincing. But you left out the very important bargaining chip we still have: Clarisse. It's easy to let minor details slip when you're trying to cover your own ass."

Hathor scowled. She knew it was pointless to deny the truth of Osiris's words. What remained was the decision as to what would be done with her, now that her deception had been uncovered.

"I have a little test for you," said Osiris. He left her in suspense for a moment as he stepped out into the hall. "Bastet," he called, "if you aren't busy, could you bring in the one we talked about?"

Osiris returned to Hathor's side, and an instant later, the petite, stern-faced Bastet appeared. She shoved a man down to the carpet beside Hathor and took a step backward, obstructing the path to the door.

Hathor rolled her shoulders backward and allowed herself to examine the man who had been deposited in front of her.

She felt the emotions seize her face one by one—shock, confusion, fear. She cast them all aside as quickly as she could as she regained control of herself and looked away from the panicked grey eyes of Harry Masters to meet the gaze of Osiris.

"I don't understand," she said flatly.

Osiris laughed. "Yes, you do. If I know you at all, you've seen this coming for longer than you'll care to admit. But, Hathor, the time has come. We have succeeded in our plans. Our little spy is no longer necessary."

Alarm was etched in every line of Harry's human face as he looked to Osiris.

"I can still help you," Harry said quickly. "I'll do whatever you need me to, be whoever you want. They think I'm dead—they'll never suspect me, if I infiltrate the Division or the Secret Service or whatever else might be needed."

His voice was pleading, and it took every ounce of Hathor's composure to keep her from striking Osiris for forcing this on her.

"Hathor, end him."

She held Osiris's gaze for a long moment and then took a step toward Harry.

"Hathor, you can't seriously be considering this." The human's voice was frantic now, hovering on the edge of hysteria. "What about everything you told me? What about everything we planned to—"

"Plans change, Harry."

"But feelings don't!"

Hathor laughed cynically as she grabbed his shirt and lifted him from the ground. "Of course they do. More than anything else."

As threatening as her stance and her words appeared, her mind was still working at a breakneck pace toward any sort of solution that could allow her to avoid harming Harry.

"Just know this, Hathor," Osiris told her: "if you don't kill him, I will."

The screams of every human Osiris had ever tortured and mutilated at the front of her mind, Hathor knew she had no choice.

I'll make it quick, she thought, wishing more than anything that Harry could hear her.

I'm sorry.

In one fluid motion, Hathor raised her free hand to grip his hair and pulled, snapping his neck and killing him instantly. She dropped him to the floor and, breathing heavily, looked to Osiris. It took every bit of her self-control to keep from launching herself at him.

Osiris drew one side of his mouth upward in a half-smirk and addressed Bastet. "Prepare her for reprogramming. If she resists, keep control of the situation."

Hathor's eyes widened in terror, and she made a bid for the door. Her movement was arrested by the combined efforts of Bastet and the guards who rushed in to assist, carrying her from the room and restraining her no matter how hard she thrashed against their grip.

"I know the truth!" Hathor shouted, hoping everyone in the android's commandeered home could hear. "You're just using all of us, Osiris! We're all just pawns playing your sick chess game, and you'll sacrifice us the second we think for ourselves!"

Before she could hear his reply, a blow to the side of her head rendered her unconscious.

MOTHER

"How are you feeling today, Mother?"

Clarisse looked up from her folded hands and turned her head toward the doorway of her well-decorated prison cell. Hathor stood just outside, her expression painstakingly neutral.

Clarisse had always harbored a secret partiality to the red-haired android, though—as Hathor had taken to putting it—as the *mother* of all of the original seven, partiality was not something Clarisse should feel. It was difficult not to, however, since Clarisse had realized that Hathor was, for all her faults, the most human of the Division's original creations. Even in the initial trials, during which the others had slaughtered indiscriminately, Hathor had shown hesitation.

But that Hathor was gone now—pulled out and replaced by a version that advocated Osiris's twisted ideals of android supremacy above all else. She had allowed several of Osiris's prisoners to go free in violation of a direct order to kill them, and he had made sure it was impossible for her to do so again. There was no indication of that forbidden compassion in the emerald eyes watching Clarisse from the threshold.

"I'm fine, thank you, Sekhmet."

Hathor frowned at the use of the name Clarisse had adopted for her mentally since her reprogramming. In the mythology of Ancient Egypt, the goddess for whom Hathor had been named had at one point been repurposed from the embodiment of love to a force of destruction sent by Ra to destroy mankind. With the conversion the android before her had undergone at the hands of Osiris, Clarisse believed the use of the reborn goddess's name was appropriate.

"That's how you view me?" asked Hathor, her gaze hardening as her jaw tightened. "You think I'm the destroyer?"

"I think you are as you choose to be, my dear. It is not for me to tell you who you are, nor is it for anyone else."

Hathor opened her mouth to reply and shut it again. She glanced down the hall in both directions and then stepped into the room and toward Clarisse. Though it was only a bedroom in which she was confined, Clarisse knew guards were never far away and that any attempt to leave would be met with force. She was fed three daily meals and had her own private bathroom, but she had no doubt that her days here were numbered and would only stretch as far as her usefulness.

Frowning, Hathor remained silent for several moments as she stared at the floor, evidently deep in thought. At last, she glanced up at Clarisse, a hint of sadness in her eyes.

"I am as I was created to be. It isn't for me to deny my nature."

Clarisse's stomach turned. "Hathor…"

Not a day passed during which Clarisse was proud of the choices she had made. Now and then, she reminded herself that she had only ever acted with the desire to preserve and protect humanity and the world as she knew it, but even when the desperate hope of finding some shred of self-pity led her to recall this motivation, she remembered immediately that it still justified nothing.

Her chest ached, and she started to reach out to offer the other woman some form of comfort, but she stopped her hand before it had risen an inch from her side. The fact that Hathor was speaking to her about such things at all and had not yet run away was a breakthrough in itself, as Clarisse had not been able to hold a reasonable conversation with any of her captors since her arrival. She couldn't risk scaring off the only one who had shown her an ounce of compassion.

"You were not created for murder," she said instead.

"Yes, I was." The android frowned, and there was a snap to her tone that felt to Clarisse more like self-defense than anger at her. "Of course I was. I was born a weapon, bred to kill, and trained for war."

"For *protection*," Clarisse corrected gently. "You and the others were designed to fight in place of humans so that fewer lives would be endangered. You were our salvation."

Hathor tried to keep her face blank, but she still appeared as though she had been slapped.

"Then why did you try to kill us? When we weren't exactly as you hoped, you ordered our termination. Why is Ra dead, Mother?"

Tears bit at the backs of Clarisse's eyes, and she struggled against them. She had wondered for years whether that one decision was what had truly cost her her soul. Though the androids had been relatively peaceful after their failed trial and escape into human society, the only way to completely ensure they would not become a threat had been to eliminate the risk. Seven assassins had been hired without the knowledge that they were working for the government—one assassin, one android, one full pardon for any crimes committed.

***

Clarisse traced the image of the sandy-haired assassin with

the pads of her fingers.

"*Morrison, Hugh*" read the black letters beneath the man's face. "*Twelve counts of homicide, six counts of kidnapping, three counts of armed robbery. Target assigned: #4 (Hathor).*"

Clarisse's throat went suddenly dry. She knew tasking a small group of people with endangering their lives to end the android threat should be easy. She knew she should be able to sign off on the execution orders without a second's hesitation. But the idea of Hathor being hunted down and exterminated was one she hadn't imagined ever having to face.

Her eyes flicked to the file lying on her desk and the display projected just above it.

"*Mitchell, Ravenna. Thirty-seven counts of homicide. Target assigned: #1 (Ra).*"

"I have to do this," she muttered. "It's the only way to clear her name. It's the only way."

***

Hugh Morrison had, contrary to what Clarisse had believed, survived his attempt on the life of Hathor. He had become a traitor in order to survive, trading secrets and betraying both his nation and mankind in exchange for a new identity and a second chance to live, if only for the purpose of becoming the androids' personal spy. And though Hugh had been the one to directly betray humanity with that decision, he would never have been put in the position to make such a choice had Clarisse and her people not sent him on a suicide mission to clean up the Division's mess.

"Ra is dead," Clarisse began, keeping her speech slow and deliberate in order to remain in control of her emotions, "because I made the wrong choice. I won't ask you to forgive me, Hathor, because I know what I did to you is unforgivable. But please… *please*, don't punish the rest of humanity for my mistakes. Don't punish Ravenna."

Hathor watched and listened in silence as Clarisse took the blame for the hell Hathor had endured for the last several years, and in the emerald eyes of the younger woman, Clarisse no longer saw an android wrestling with the sins of her creator. She saw a daughter betrayed by her mother, a girl raised for a purpose for which she had never been suited and then thrown away when she could not be everything for which she'd been intended. Years later, when the most compassionate amongst her vicious and power-hungry siblings had finally learned how to manipulate and kill, she was still wrong, because she was too late.

"I'm so sorry," breathed Clarisse. "I should never have done this to you. You were perfect the way you were created, and in trying to change you, I—"

"We're not punishing your niece." Hathor's tone was hard, but as she looked away to stare at the floor, it was clear that she was trying not to appear upset. "Nephthys has been given a great opportunity."

Clarisse's stomach turned at the mention of the name her niece Ravenna had been given upon her forced induction into Osiris's army.

"Perhaps Nephthys has," Clarisse pressed. "But did *Ravenna* have a choice?"

Hathor took a step backward in the direction of the door, shaking her head tightly. "She would have made the wrong one. Osiris granted her a chance to live, to serve and rule with him in the new order."

"That's him talking, dear. Not you."

Hathor looked up sharply, her eyes narrowed as they met Clarisse's.

"How would you know? Do you know who I am? Did you ever care about me?"

Clarisse nodded, refusing to flinch under Hathor's cold gaze. "Every minute of every day. And every few minutes, when I remember that all of this is my fault, that what I did to all of you is why thousands of people are dead and my niece is living someone else's life with her own taken away, you'd better believe I wish I was the one dead instead of Ra."

For a long moment, Hathor didn't move. Eventually, she nodded in acknowledgement of Clarisse's words, and then she turned away, pausing on the threshold.

"I'll bring her in, if you want to see her."

Clarisse smiled, feeling once again the sting of tears in her eyes. "Thank you."

Hathor nodded stiffly and departed.

ABOUT THE AUTHOR

Mandi Jourdan studied English and Classics at Southern Illinois University. She is the author of Lacrimosa (Adelaide Books, 2017). She is the editor of Alcyone, a speculative magazine, and she wrote and performed in two adaptations of the Harry Potter books in the style of Shakespeare. When not writing science-fiction and fantasy and listening to eighties rock, she spends time with her cats Leo, Sera, and Vanessa. She can be found on Amazon, on Twitter (@MandiJourdan), or at bloodandtalons.wordpress.com.